With special thanks to Laurie J. Edwards

First published in 2014 by Curious Fox,
an imprint of Capstone Global Library Limited,
7 Pilgrim Street, London, EC4V 6LB
Registered company number: 6695582

www.curious-fox.com

Text © Hothouse Fiction Ltd 2014

Series created by Hothouse Fiction
www.hothousefiction.com

The author's moral rights are hereby asserted.

Cover design by Steve Mead. Photographs by Studio8.

ISBN 978 1 78202 077 6

18 17 16 15 14
1 3 5 7 9 10 8 6 4 2

A CIP catalogue for this book is available from the British Library.

Typeset in Adobe Garamond Pro by Hothouse Fiction Ltd

Printed and bound by CPI Group (UK) Ltd, Croydon, CRO 4YY

This book is presented purely for entertainment purposes. While the
Wanted series has its basis in the Wild West of Arizona in the 1880s,
the places, people and events have been fictionalized.

MIX
Paper from
responsible sources
FSC® C020471
www.fsc.org

To all those rough-riding CPs who saddled up and galloped along with me on this journey

CHAPTER ONE

Grace felt her heartbeat quicken with a spark of panic as she ran towards her brother, watching the horse rear and whinny as it dragged him by the lead rope. Daniel flew into the air and fell down hard in a cloud of dust. Bullet reared again, his eyes wild and darting, his hooves stamping inches from Daniel's head. Her throat tightened, but she kept her voice steady.

"Let go of the rope. Roll to your right."

Daniel quickly curled into a ball and rolled away. She gave a shrill whistle and Bullet wheeled round to charge across the yard straight for her, but Grace held her ground and he skidded to a halt, flanks heaving.

She grabbed the swaying rope. "It's OK, boy." She reached

out slowly, making sure Bullet's gaze followed her hand before she patted his neck. "Calm down."

"Everything all right out there?" Pa shouted from inside the barn. The whinnying and crashing in there sounded like he was having his own problems with the mustangs.

Daniel got up, wincing, and looked pleadingly at her. Pa had strict rules about an eleven-year-old going near an unbroken horse like Bullet, and Daniel had disobeyed all of them.

"Fine, Pa," Grace answered.

Daniel grinned and began examining the rope burn on his palms. Grace looked him up and down for injuries, but apart from a bruised ego, he was OK. Her brother loved horses as much as she did, but hadn't learned the firm yet gentle approach needed for a wild horse. He hitched up his sleeve, examining a couple of scratches. There'd be a few more before he got it, but she knew he would. Every Milton was as stubborn as the horses they tamed, though none of them would admit it.

She led Bullet into the paddock, patted his rump and watched him take off across their piece of desert. Daniel's hat lay in the dirt near the corral fence and she picked it up, dusting off the worst marks, before handing it over to him. He put it on and frowned, watching Bullet canter along the skyline. Grace shook her head at his frustrated expression.

"Even Pa can't get near Bullet," Grace said.

"But *you* can." He kicked at the dirt.

She shrugged. "I couldn't do it when I was your age."

Of course, they'd still lived on the East Coast then, but Daniel didn't need to know that. "Takes time."

When they'd arrived in Arizona to homestead, Grace had never expected to fall in love with this red clay and rock desert, dotted with tall columns of saguaro and spiny branches of ocotillo, but now she felt she belonged in the West.

The noise inside the stable quieted, and a few minutes later Pa emerged, caked in sweat.

"Those mustangs will be tough to break." He was tired, but she could hear the relish in his voice for the challenge. He nodded at her. "Good job today."

He glanced at Daniel's burned palms but said nothing, and she bit her lip to stop herself from smiling. Nothing got past Pa.

Behind him, the sun dipped low on the horizon, tipping the Dragoon Mountains with orange fire and streaking the scrubby tufts of grass golden. No dust clouds appeared on the road that stretched between their ranch and the distant town of Tombstone. She caught Pa looking for them too. Riders churned up puffs of grit when they made that half-day trip to the ranch, and her family didn't get many friendly visitors.

Lately the threats had been getting worse.

She followed her father and brother over to the pump, where they washed up. Then they stomped the muck from their boots and stepped through the open doorway of the log cabin. Grace hung her hat on a peg by the door and smoothed back the strands of long blonde hair that had escaped from her braid.

Two-year-old Abby toddled over and tugged at Grace's legs. Ma had cut down a pair of Pa's old leggings for Grace to wear under her calico dress – she'd grown out of it over a year ago, but they had no money for new clothes as every penny went into the horse ranch. It would be worth it though: in one more year they'd own their land outright. If only their land wasn't so highly sought after and they didn't keep hearing rumours of ranch owners forced out. There were also Indian attacks to worry about…

She picked up Abby, feeling the burn in her muscles from the day's work, and settled her on one hip. Abby beamed and chattered away to her cornhusk doll in a language known only to her.

Ma's face was flushed from bending over the iron pot hanging in the hearth, and she wiped her hands on the flour-sack apron tied over her gingham dress. Steam rose from the bubbling broth and the tang of leeks perfumed the air. With the fire going, it almost felt hotter inside than it had been under the blazing sun earlier. Already used to the heat, Zeke slept soundly in the hand-carved cradle near the hearth, one fist clenched.

"Supper's almost ready," said Ma, as Pa wrapped his arms around her.

"Good. I'm as hungry as a horse," he said, giving her

a swift kiss.

Ma laughed. "Daniel, go get some hay for your father's dinner."

"You mean it?"

Grace rubbed her knuckles over her brother's head. "Come help me set the table."

Still balancing Abby on one hip, Grace handed bowls and spoons to Daniel, who thumped them down on the table quickly. When they were done, she settled Abby on the bench and began to slice the cornbread.

Ma poured Pa a drink and handed it to him as he stretched out in a chair. "What do you plan to do about that deed, Bill?" she asked in a low voice.

"If the Guiltless Gang think they can…" Pa's voice dropped to a whisper. Grace leaned closer to hear, but Ma held up a hand to stop his words.

"Daniel, bring in more branches for the fire. And Grace, I need you to fetch more potatoes and carrots for the soup."

Grace sighed. Ma was still treating her like her younger siblings – maybe they hadn't picked up on the tense atmosphere lately, but *she* had. She dawdled, hoping Pa would start talking again before she went outside.

"*Now*, Grace." Ma issued the command in her obey-or-else voice.

Grace trudged outside to the root cellar, which was dug into the ground a few feet from the side of the house.

She tugged on the handle to lift the hatch door and, holding the door up with one hand, started down the rough-hewn steps that led into the darkness. A sharp scent of garlic and onion mingled with the earthiness of potatoes and rutabagas wafted from the cavernous underground space.

As she carried on into the musty cellar, her boot toe struck something and sent it clattering down the stone steps. She swore, safely away from Ma's ears, realizing she'd kicked the long wooden stick they used to prop the cellar door open. It would be almost impossible to find in the slivers of dying daylight from the slatted cellar door. Inching her way down into the stone-lined pit after it, she struggled to keep the hinged lid open with one outstretched arm. The moist air cooled the sweat that had begun to bead on her brow as she peered into the dark. But then the sole of her leather boot slid across the damp stone and she fell the last few steps, smacking her funny bone. The hatch slammed shut overhead, shrouding her in darkness. Pain radiated through her arm and vibrated through her clenched teeth, and she lay on the wet dirt and cradled her elbow, groaning.

Suddenly, the sound of thunder shook the ground above her. No, not thunder. Pounding hooves. Whooping and hollering filled the air. *A stampede from behind the ranch? Or an Indian attack? How could that be?* She hadn't seen the tell-tale kick-up of dust in the distance. They must have come from another direction.

Her heart thumped against her ribs as she scrambled up the steps and pushed on the heavy door with one hand. She strained her muscles, but the hatch didn't budge. It was wedged shut.

Before she could call out, the crack of a rifle bounced off the stone walls and echoed in the hollowness behind her. Grace gasped, but the noise caught in her throat. The thundering hooves quieted to stamping. A horse snorted close by. Whoever had ridden in was almost overhead.

"William Milton, you signed that deed yet?"

Pa's boots clomped across the wooden porch of the house. Her fists clenched when she heard the tremor in his answer. "This ranch is mine, Elijah Hale."

A muffled, mirthless laugh. "That so?"

Stirrups jingled and heavy footsteps tramped across the ground towards the house. There was the sound of a scuffle overhead. Grace's mouth went dry. *What's going on?* She shoved again at the wooden hatch with both hands, ignoring the pain shooting through her throbbing elbow. *Open! Just open!* Grace pleaded silently, but it was stuck fast.

"NO!" came Pa's strangled cry. "Don't hurt her!"

Don't hurt who? A bubble of panic rose inside Grace. *Are the men hurting Ma? Abby?*

"You had your chance." The voice was cold and emotionless.

"Don't!" Pa sounded desperate and he was panting hard. "Take the horses, the ranch, whatever you want."

"Oh, we'll take them all right."

A shot rang out.

Pa moaned: a keening sound from the depth of his being. She heard Ma break down sobbing. *Abby? They couldn't have...* Grace felt sick to her stomach, tears stinging her eyes; everything was happening too quickly, yet the sound of the gunshot was still ringing in her ears.

She took two steps up, gritted her teeth and thrust her shoulder against the hatch, feeling nothing at first except the force of the door weighing down on her. But then finally it gave and she had to stop quickly, before it flung open. Palms shining with sweat, she carefully lifted the door an inch.

As the air outside the cellar hit her, her arms trembled so much she almost dropped the hatch door. There was a scorched smell – a sickening odour of burnt flesh and the sulphurous stench of discharged gunpowder. In the commotion, no one had noticed the cellar door lifting.

She could see her sister lying on the ground, not moving.

Daniel ran up to the house, calling out to Ma. Grace's heart broke. Her little brother's voice, that she'd heard boisterous, excited, even delirious with the fever, had never sounded so small. One of the men unsheathed his knife and Grace squeezed her eyes shut on instinct, hearing Daniel's cry of surprise, then the thud of his body against the dusty earth.

Nausea rolled over her in waves. Heat prickled over her body and saliva built up in her mouth, making her want

14

to spit, want to lean over and heave, but she didn't dare make a sound.

Suddenly Ma broke free from the man holding her and ran towards the children. The man with the drooping moustache quickly glanced at Hale and received a nod. He took aim with his gun and Grace nearly shouted out, but Pa got there first.

"Eliza!"

Ma looked up, tears streaming down her face, and their eyes met.

The man pulled the trigger.

In case Pa made a similar move, two gang members stepped forward – one wrenched Pa's arms behind his back, the other bound them tightly. Pa, weakened with grief, put up no resistance. He couldn't stop staring at the heap of crumpled gingham.

Grace forced herself to look away. She had to do something. *Move! Get a weapon. Anything.*

If only she had a gun, she'd shoot the whole gang dead without a second thought. She glanced about frantically for a weapon in the dark cellar and her eyes finally fell upon the stick, lying at the foot of the steps. It was all she had. Grace lowered the hatch lid as gently as she could, closing it off against the horror above her. She went quietly down the steps into the blackness and ran her hands over the stone floor until her fingers closed around the stick. Snatching it up, she scrambled back up the steps on her hands and knees. If she caught someone by surprise, maybe she *could* grab a gun...

She pushed her shoulder against the hatch again until it lifted a bit, and then peered out cautiously. A short distance away, Hale bent over Daniel's unmoving body, a smile of satisfaction on his lips.

"Shame, such young 'uns." A woman's voice came from directly overhead and startled Grace so much that she almost dropped the hatch door. Although she craned her neck, all she could see through the crack in the hatch was the forelegs of an Appaloosa and a snakeskin boot with a stovepipe top and a snake design stitched into it. Custom-made boots, not the kind most ranchers wore, and a smaller size than Grace's own feet.

"Going soft, Bella?" Hale taunted. "We can't leave no witnesses."

As if to emphasize his point, he gave Daniel a swift kick with his boot.

Fury twisted Grace's insides. She tensed, poised to explode from the cellar and knock that grin from his face.

But from across the yard, Pa wriggled frantically on the ground where they had dumped him. He was unable to signal with his bound arms or legs, but his movement drew her gaze. Their eyes locked, then he glanced quickly over to his captors, who were still watching Hale's gloating. Grace suppressed the roar of rage rumbling within her and concentrated on Pa. He was trying to tell her something.

Slowly, almost imperceptibly, her father shook his head. His mouth silently formed the words "Stay put". He flicked his chin towards the house. He wanted her to stay hidden, because there was still Zeke to protect. So far, he hadn't cried.

Grace clenched her teeth. Standing by was almost more than she could bear, but Pa's pleading eyes kept her quiet. Her fingers stayed tight around the stick as Hale barked out another order.

"Search the house," he shouted. "Bring any stray young 'uns out here."

A couple of the men went inside, and Grace panicked, wondering if Ma had had time to hide Zeke.

Just then, Hale turned and began to stalk lazily towards the cellar. He was headed straight for her. *So be it*, she thought. She braced herself for whatever might come next.

Then Pa's voice rang out. "Hale."

Hale's steps faltered. He glanced over his shoulder. "You talking to me?"

Pa snarled, "I sure am, you low-down, yellow-bellied coward."

No, Pa, don't provoke him, Grace screamed silently.

Hale whirled, one hand on his gun.

Pa kept on. "You're a dandified city slicker with no *guts*."

Hale's laugh held the meanness of a rabid dog as he gestured towards the bleeding bodies of her family. "That the act of a coward?"

"Yes," her father said through gritted teeth. "A coward who lets others do his killing for him."

In one swift movement, Hale whipped his revolver from his holster.

Grace clamped a hand over her mouth and squeezed her eyes shut as the gun's sharp report ricocheted. The sound reverberated off the stones and seemed to rip straight through her heart.

When she finally opened her eyes, Pa lay motionless beside Ma.

Elijah Hale glanced around. "Anyone else got something to say?"

No one answered him.

Grace stared at her parents' lifeless bodies, hardly able to breathe. Her father had sacrificed his life for hers. She *had* to stay alive for him and get to Zeke, or this hell would have been for nothing. Fierce tears burned in her eyes, but she knew one thing: Hale had been wrong when he'd said "no witnesses". Her arm ached with the strain of holding the door aloft only a crack, but in the dying light of the sun she imprinted every single detail of the Guiltless Gang's faces into her memory. The man with pockmarked cheeks and a scraggly beard, and the other with a similar build but a clean-shaven face and slicked-back hair. Another, squinty eyes with a drooping moustache. The ruthless knife-wielder with the hawk-like nose. The woman with the custom snakeskin boots. All of them.

And Grace would *never* forget Elijah Hale's face. It would haunt her nightmares.

He glanced at the bodies of her family.

"One place we still didn't check though..." he said.

Hale strode back towards the cellar, his gun still clenched in his fist.

CHAPTER TWO

Grace's eyes widened and she gritted her teeth, trying desperately to stiffen her arm, but she couldn't steady the hatch lid. She thought about letting it close, but she had to know what was happening above her. If Hale was coming to check the cellar, she was as good as dead anyway. As he stalked towards her hiding place, her heart stuttered the way it had once when she'd surprised a rattlesnake – but the cruelty in Hale's eyes terrified her more than any rattler poised to strike.

Part of her wanted to back away into the darkness, try to hide, even bury herself under the vegetables… But she couldn't. If the gang were searching, they would find her soon enough, and if she was going to die, she would not die a coward.

Grace gritted her teeth, ready to pop the hatch door into Hale's face when he leaned down to open it.

His spurs jingled with each step closer. Six paces away.

Five… Four…

"We better move out!"

Hale stopped as one of his men galloped around from the side of the cabin, shouting. It was the man who'd killed Daniel. Bile rose in her throat, and she crouched to see his face more clearly. He was clean-shaven, and the bandana tied around his neck was as black as his eyes.

"Pretty Boy already done set the place on fire," he said.

Hale spun and spat. "Grab some of the horses first."

Relief coursed through Grace when Hale changed direction and strode quickly towards the paddock, but her body still trembled uncontrollably. She could just make out curls of smoke beginning to rise from the far corner of the cabin.

Zeke!

If her baby brother was still safe, she had to find a way to get to him. Her eyes darted furtively left to right, watching for an opportunity. Greying twilight silhouetted the men as they ran towards the stable, and chaos whirled above her hiding place – horses whinnying, Hale's men swearing, hooves stamping. The slap of saddles being thrown on horseback, reins jangling as horses were yanked viciously into a group.

"Let them wild ones go!" the man with the drooping moustache shouted. "They's nothing but trouble."

The freed mustangs bolted from the barn, heading for the hills, and Grace choked on the clouds of dust kicked up by their hooves as they stampeded past the cracked cellar hatch door. All her father's work, for nothing. As two of the men tossed tack and equipment into a heap by the stable, the ache in her chest grew.

One whinny stood out from the rest of the bedlam.

Bullet! Please don't let them take Bullet...

Keeping the hatch lid steady, Grace squatted lower to keep an eye on the horse, swallowing hard as Hale opened the paddock gate. He lunged at Bullet, grabbing for the halter, and the stallion pulled back his lips, revealing his teeth. He snapped out at Hale, who stepped back to avoid the horse's chomping jaws. Grace cheered silently as Hale was unable to get close.

He stormed away and vaulted the fence. Mounting his own horse, Hale galloped back to the paddock gate. "Toss me a lead," he shouted to the nearest man, who was loaded down with tack.

The man threw him a rope and Hale caught it in one hand, then charged towards Bullet. Bringing his pinto alongside, Hale leaned out from his saddle and grabbed for Bullet's halter again, but the palomino screamed and reared, his hoof clipping Hale in the face. He tumbled from his horse and landed in a heap as Bullet flew towards the open gate. Hale sat up quickly, clutching his cheek. Blood trickled through his fingers, and

Grace felt her lips twist into a bitter smile.

"Stop that horse!" he snarled.

"Just let it go." The woman's voice came from somewhere above Grace's head again. She must have already mounted her Appaloosa – Grace could see its hooves stamping impatiently right outside the root cellar's hatch. An icy chill slithered down her spine. They were so close to her – what if Hale remembered his intention to search the cellar?

"We need to go." Her voice was strained. The Appaloosa edged past the opening.

Hale staggered to his feet and went for his gun.

Bullet rounded the stable at a gallop and, before Hale could aim properly, wove back and forth between the saguaro, heading straight out for the mountains. Grace clenched her teeth and willed Bullet to go faster.

At least one of us should get away from here...

After an unbearable delay, the Guiltless Gang finally galloped off in a clatter of hooves, neighs, and churning sand. Grace peered out from her hiding place, staring into the gathering night as, like spokes on a wagon wheel, the gang fanned out in different directions. Within moments they'd disappeared into the blackness.

As soon as the hoof beats faded, Grace burst from

the root cellar.

Zeke. Save Zeke.

The thought pulsed through her as urgently as her heartbeat. Tongues of flame were already licking the night sky behind the cabin, and smoke rose from the back corner. The gang had set the woodpile on fire, but at least the heavy logs chinked with adobe caught more slowly. On shaky limbs, Grace stumbled towards the door to the cabin, but in her haste she tripped on the step and slammed her knee against the porch. Ignoring the pain, she scrambled to her feet, rushed to the door and yanked it open.

Her stomach lurched. Overturned furniture. Chairs flung in a jumbled heap against the log walls, legs snapped off. Bedding slashed. Crockery smashed on the floor.

And the upended cradle splintered against the stone hearth.

"Z-Zeke...?" Grace said hoarsely.

Burning wood spit and crackled like gunshots, and a second later, the straw ticking mattress in the back corner of the cabin burst into flames. She dropped to her knees, panic clawing at her insides as she bunched up her skirt and crawled across the floor, searching desperately amongst the broken furniture. She ducked low to stay beneath the billowing smoke, dodging the shooting sparks. She had to find Zeke.

Fire ate along the back wall, consuming the chairs. Ma's overturned soup pot had doused the embers in the fireplace, and broth had soaked into the dirt by the hearth. Bits and

24

pieces of vegetables lay scattered on the dirt floor. Tears stung Grace's eyes. She remembered Ma stirring the soup for the dinner they would never have.

Don't think about it. Find Zeke. Now.

Grace dug furiously through the broken cradle slats, flinging them behind her. Trapped under the shattered cradle, she came across the tintype photograph Ma kept on the hearth – it must have fallen to the ground in the confusion. Grace snatched up the only picture of her family and quickly tucked it inside her bodice before returning to her task, tearing at the cracked headboard of her brother's crib. The pointed iron edges of the tintype scratched her skin, but she hardly noticed. She finally moved the last of the wood away, and sucked down the sob that rose in her throat as she saw what she'd exposed.

Zeke lay on the floor.

Grace rocked back onto her heels, and acrid smoke choked her as she stared at Zeke's motionless body.

She started suddenly as the back corner of the roof caved in, and smoke quickly swirled towards them. She didn't have time now to check if he was alive or dead. Scooping her brother up, she tucked him against her with one arm. Crouching low, she arched her upper body over Zeke's to protect him from falling debris as the smoke curled lower, and then crawled one-armed towards the door, her lungs burning with each breath. Grit and ash filled her mouth, scratching her throat, and she slapped at sparks on her dress and skin.

By the time she reached the porch, the knees of her leggings were shredded. Gasping with relief at getting outside, Grace gulped ragged breaths into her air-starved lungs and then, gripping her brother, stood up and raced from the cabin towards open pasture a safe distance from the caving timbers. She collapsed into a sitting position against the rough wood of a fence post, coughing and panting hard. The darkness of the evening was illuminated by the roaring fire, shedding flickering light on the nightmare all around them.

Finally, reluctantly, Grace looked down at her brother's limp body, reaching out a tentative hand and placing it on Zeke's chest. For one moment, she thought her hand rose with his breath, and her heart expanded until her own chest ached.

He's alive?

Hope filled her for a brief instant, but the crackle of flames, imploding walls, and plumes of smoke rising into the night sky brought reality hurtling back. She closed her eyes and the fire's heat seared her eyelids as terrifying visions danced in her mind. The rest of her family were lying dead, their bodies scattered around her in the smoke-filled yard. Grace hugged the baby fiercely to her body. "It's going to be OK, Zeke. It's going to be OK…"

If someone had seen the smoke, maybe the law would come and they'd be all right? She struggled to draw more air into her tortured lungs, choking and coughing in the drifting haze. She had to get up, back farther away from the fire, but her muscles had gone rubbery. She had no strength, no energy, no willpower.

And, as she looked down again at Zeke, she realized he remained unmoving, his eyes still closed.

"No! No. No. No…" she whispered, her voice just a croak. She laid her ear against his chest. Silent and still. Not even a whisper of breath. Not even a faint heartbeat.

He hadn't made it.

Numbness crept through her. Nobody was coming to save them. Grace slumped against the fence with Zeke still lying in her lap, staring into the distance as his body grew stiff and cold, and the cabin crumbled into ash. Her will to live drained away, leaving behind only a soulless, empty shell.

A coyote howled nearby, echoing around in the air like the wail of a ghost.

With Zeke's body still clasped in her arms, Grace sprang to her feet, as if it was a call to action. Her family. She had to bury them – now, before the animals circled for them. She could at least give them that.

Cradling Zeke in one arm, she scrabbled in the loose sand with her other hand, carving out a hole – but as fast as she dug, sand on the edges trickled back in, filling the opening.

Setting Zeke gently on the ground, Grace ran a hand

over his curls and then reached into her bodice to pull out the tintype so its sharp iron edges wouldn't poke her as she worked. She placed it beside her baby brother, then she began to dig like a dog, shooting the sand behind her – but two feet down, she struck hard-baked clay.

A shovel. She needed a shovel.

Grace stood, a little unsure on her feet at first, and then rushed to the stable. She rooted through the jumbled pile the gang had left behind and found the manure shovel. Returning to the hole, she attacked the ground with a vengeance. Stomping on the edge of the blade, Grace sent the shovel deep into the resistant clay, twisting out chunks the way she wished she could twist a knife into the heart of every one of those murderers.

The pit grew deeper, wider, but she didn't stop. The moon rose higher in the sky. She kept digging. Her hands blistered. She kept digging. The blisters oozed clear liquid. Still she dug. Just before greyness edged over the horizon, she finally flung away the shovel. She had to finish this in the dark – she couldn't bear it in the light. The pit was deep now, but it would never be deep enough to bury the horror of what had happened there.

Her palms raw, she tugged at the bodies of her family, dragging them to the pit one by one to bury them all together. She placed Pa in there first. Then Ma, with Abby beside her. Tugging Daniel by the boots, she settled him beside their sister.

Darkness obscured her family's features, but their faces smiled at her from memory. Realizing that Daniel's hat must have fallen off, Grace backtracked and found it. She leaned down into the pit to set the hat over his face.

"There you go, pardner."

She choked back her tears and pulled herself up. Only Zeke was left. Grace sank to the grass beside him, taking him into her arms and rocking his body back and forth again as deep sobs wracked her body, flowing up from her shattered heart in tidal waves. Eventually, she nestled him into the curve of Ma's arm.

"Goodbye," she whispered.

Scoop and toss. Scoop and toss. Scoop and toss. Each shovelful a prayer. A vow. A promise for justice. She was burying her family, and burying her old life. Grace mounded the clay into a small hill, packing it down as a barrier against coyotes or other wild animals that might steal the bones. Bile rose again in her throat at the very thought.

She needed a marker. A cross. Grace glanced around at the bits of splintered wood that lay on the ground near the cabin's smouldering ruins. The pieces were crooked, with edges as jagged as her heart, and as she went over and picked up a shard, a splinter jabbed into her finger but she barely felt it. Realizing she needed rope to secure the cross, she picked up Bullet's lead rope, which still swung from the paddock fence. She'd never use it again. She wound it around the wooden arms to hold them together, tied it off, and then reached down to pick up the tintype she'd laid aside.

Grace climbed the mound with the cross in hand, and with the back of the shovel she drove it into the hard-packed clay. Then she lay down next to the cross and clasped the picture of her family tightly in her hand, so hard that the iron edges bit into her raw and blistered skin. Shivers wracked her body, waves of grief rippling from the inside out, and cold froze her tears into an icy block in her chest, constricting her breathing.

Why did I survive? Why am I still alive?

She knew why.

To get justice.

She had a new purpose now, and she wouldn't rest until the same fate befell the Guiltless Gang as had befallen each of her loved ones. Grace got to her feet and made her way down the curved mound under which her family lay, then stood gazing at the cross pointing towards the sky. The clay mound echoed the shape of the distant mountains. Mountains that rose solid and sure.

Slivers of pink now streaked the horizon. The earth kept spinning, but the world she had known stopped here, forever.

Grace tucked the tintype back into her bodice and pressed it against her heart while she sat watching the sun rise, the emptiness in her chest deeper than the pit she had dug. She had no idea what to do now. The old Grace lay beneath the ground with the family she loved. She would never be the same again...

Something cold and wet nudged her arm, and she jumped. A familiar huff followed.

Bullet?

She must be dreaming. But the palomino snorted again, and tossed his mane as she turned to face him. When she didn't respond more, Bullet moved closer and blew his breath into her face. Finally she leaped to her feet and threw her arms around his neck, her chest growing tight once more as she buried her face in his mane.

Bullet had come back for her. She wasn't alone.

Pulling back from him, she gritted her teeth.

"This isn't over," she murmured. Suddenly, she had a thought. "Wait here, boy."

Striding over to the barn, Grace rooted through the debris the gang had left behind, fearing they'd taken what she was looking for. But then, hidden under piles of hay, she found the tin. Her father had hidden this old gun here in case of any rattlers or sudden Indian attacks. If only he'd had a chance to get to it before... She pushed the thought away. Opening the metal box, she reached inside and closed her hand around the smooth handle of her father's old Colt revolver. She slid it out and stared at it, her finger testing the trigger. Pa had shown her how to use it, telling her how he'd wrestled it away from a soldier. If it had been hidden down in the root cellar, maybe none of this would have happened. If only.

Swallowing hard, Grace flipped open the cylinder. There were only three bullets inside, but no matter. She'd find more if she had to. Tucking the gun into the waistband of her skirt and covering it with her bodice, she dug through the piles until she'd found a worn-out saddle, shabby reins, scuffed saddlebags, and a hide water pouch that had been discarded in the commotion. Striding back to Bullet, she strapped them on and mounted.

Together they'd see that justice was done.

The Guiltless would hang.

CHAPTER THREE

As the morning wore on and the sun rose higher over the hills, Grace leaned into Bullet's canter. The blisters on her palms, raw and oozing, stung in the whistling wind. Her father's gun, hidden in her waistband, dug into her back. Bullet's mane whipped into her face, but the warmth and closeness of her horse did not ease the hard knot of grief deep in her gut. Every inch of her body felt numb, though the pounding of Bullet's hooves jarred her body the way reality battered her heart.

Each hoof beat was a denial. *No. It can't be. This is a nightmare. It isn't real. No. No. No.* The rhythm echoed in her brain.

"Faster," she whispered against Bullet's neck. As if he'd

understood her, the palomino picked up speed. Fury fuelled her ride. She'd make them pay. Every last one of them. She needed to find the sheriff.

By the time they reached Allen Street, the main road in town, Bullet's coat was lathered with sweat and Grace's throat was parched. She slowed him to a walk.

Heads swivelled to follow her progress through the street, making her conscious of her ill-fitting, outgrown clothes. The bloody stains on the hem of her skirt. The torn leggings underneath. The red clay caking her boots. The ash and soot streaking her bodice and her sweaty face. Her cheeks burned with shame. Grace funnelled her embarrassment into her thirst for justice. *I* will *see those murderers hanged*, she vowed again silently.

Before she reached his office, she spotted the sheriff, his badge glinting in the sunlight as he sauntered across the street and entered the Bird Cage Theatre. Grace reined in Bullet and headed that way.

Every time she had come to town with her family, Pa had crossed the street to avoid the Bird Cage. When she was younger, Grace had been fascinated by the painted ladies in their revealing dresses, their petticoats showing, flouncing through the doors. Some of the bolder women took men's arms to lead them inside the pink building. A few men shook off the painted ladies' claws, but others smiled and accompanied the women inside. Now that she was older, Grace understood why

Pa had shied away.

Pointedly ignoring the stares of passers-by, Grace slid from Bullet's back. After looping the reins around a post at the edge of the wooden sidewalk, she stiffened her back and lifted her chin. The planks vibrated under her boots as she strode to the Bird Cage's door. But with one hand on the ornate brass doorknob, she hesitated. No decent woman would enter such a place. Dishevelled as she was and in her too-small clothing, people might think…

But then a host of terrible images flashed through her mind. Her mother's lifeless body, next to Abby's. The gunshot. Pa's body falling. Zeke's limp, lifeless form.

The open grave.

A sob rose in her throat, but she swallowed it down.

The sheriff was in there – she had to go inside. Justice for her family mattered more than her reputation.

"I'm sorry, Pa," she whispered. Then, taking a deep breath, she opened the door.

Clouds of smoke enveloped her. Not the black acrid smoke from the burning cabin still clinging to her pores and clothes, but sweetish cigar smoke and the sharper scent of burning tobacco from hand-rolled cigarettes. Raucous laughter, the tinkle of a piano, and the clink of glass pulsed through the room. The infamous alcoves, or birdcages, some with their red velvet curtains drawn, perched overhead like rows of fancy packages.

Her eyes stinging from the haze, Grace squinted to find the sheriff. So many black frock coats blurred into an indistinguishable mass.

A deep voice purred from behind her. "Looking for someone, darling?"

She shook off the paw resting on her shoulder. "The sheriff." Her voice came out clipped, curt.

"Not a very friendly one, are you now?" The whisky on the cowboy's breath overpowered her as he rounded her to get a better look. "Bit young for this business, aren't ya?"

"My only *business*" – Grace glared as she emphasized the word – "is with the sheriff."

"Lucky man." The cowboy eyed Grace's threadbare bodice. "But I don't envy him the sharp edge of your tongue." He waved toward a table in the dark corner of the room. "Better catch him now before he gets involved in *other* business."

When Grace turned toward the corner, the cowboy latched onto her arm. "Want me to escort you?"

He may have been expecting a simpering painted lady but Grace had been breaking wild horses for the past four years. She yanked her elbow back sharply and was not sorry when it connected with his gut.

Breath whooshed from his lungs. He bent over, clutching his stomach. "You little…" he gasped.

But Grace was already striding toward the table where the sheriff was nursing a drink and talking to a buxom older lady

36

in a frilled skirt.

"Sheriff, I apologize for interrupting." Heat flushed Grace's cheeks as she caught sight of the woman's rouged face, her exposed cleavage, and the ruffled hemline of her dress, which rose higher in the front than Grace's outgrown skirt. "I-I'm sorry, ma'am, but I must talk to the sheriff. It's urgent."

The woman nodded, the red feathers in her hair bobbing with each movement. She squeezed the sheriff's shoulder. "I'll be ready whenever you are, Johnny." The undercurrents in her light, teasing tone made Grace cringe.

"Sheriff Behan at your service." The heavy-set man waved a casual hand toward his badge. "So, what can I do for you, Miss—"

"Grace Milton, sir."

"Have a seat, Miz Milton." He started to stand.

Grace hastily dragged out the nearest chair and plopped into it. Not very graceful, but what she had to say was too urgent to wait for the usual manners.

"And what can I do for you?"

"Yesterday my parents … my whole family…" Grace's tongue tripped over the words. If she said them, it would make it real. But if she didn't, those killers would get away with what they'd done. Grace drew in a breath and started again. "The Guiltless Gang. They … *murdered* my parents. And my brothers and sister." *Don't fall apart. Tell him the whole story. Get justice.* She rushed on. "Elijah Hale. He was the leader. He

37

… he shot my pa."

The sheriff's face paled at the mention of Hale's name. "Uh… Well now, them's pretty serious accusations you're bringing against Mr Hale." He leaned back in his chair and steepled his fingers, though his hands shook slightly. "He's well known in these parts as a respectable man."

Respectable man? Fury clouded Grace's eyesight. She pinched her lips together to control her tongue and temper. A picture of Hale imprinted itself in her mind; Hale striding forward, his gun pointed toward her father's heart.

The sheriff pulled a cigar from his vest pocket. He rolled it between his fingers, avoiding her eyes.

Grace clenched the wooden chair arms to stop her hands from shaking. The roughened wood tore at her tender, blistered palms and reminded her of last night. Moisture pooled in her eyes and she blinked to prevent it from spilling down her cheeks. *Stick to the facts. You can cry later.* "Did you hear me? Elijah Hale *killed* my pa."

The sheriff stuck one end of the cigar into the side of his mouth. He chomped down, twisted, and then spat the end into the nearby spittoon. The wad hit the brass with a wet ringing sound. He shifted the cigar in his mouth and then said around it, "Any witnesses?"

The nerve of the man! "Me!" Grace choked out. "I saw it *all*."

Sheriff Behan concentrated on lighting the end of the cigar. Then he blew a puff of smoke in Grace's direction. "Not sure your word" – his gaze raked her dishevelled form – "would stand up against Hale's. He's one of the richest men round these parts." He waved his cigar in a dismissive circle. "You bring me some *proof*, and I'll reconsider."

A white-hot volcano of rage erupted in Grace's stomach. Did that badge glinting at her across the table mean anything at all?

"Proof? Our cabin's burned to the ground and … and…" Grace bit her lip to hold back a cloudburst of tears. She couldn't let him see any more weakness. "My family's dead in the ground too." She sucked in air to control the tremor in her voice, but choked on cigar fumes. "I dug their graves myself." She held out her blistered and bloodied hands. "Is that proof enough for you?"

Something flickered in the sheriff's eyes. Pity maybe? But he quickly shuttered it. "Well now, that's a sad story, but it's one I've heard before." He shifted the cigar from one side of his mouth to the other and leaned back in his chair again. Behan continued, his voice loaded with fake sympathy. "Lots of Injuns round here. Understandable that you'd be a mite mixed up following such a tragedy." He nodded. "You being hysterical and all. Yep, an easy mistake to make."

"I. Am. Not. Hysterical." Grace spat out each word. *Furious, yes. Hysterical, no*. Although he was fast driving her toward loss of control. She'd kept a tight rein on her emotions when she'd wanted to scream, cry, rage. She'd tamped down the agony, struggled to come across as level-headed. If she unleashed her fury now, he'd use it against her. He'd have witnesses that she'd come unhinged. Oh, what she'd like to do to him…

Grace shoved back her chair and stood. She'd get no help from this snake. But she would not let him patronize her. "If you won't do your duty, I'll … I'll…" What could she do? No one here would help her if he wouldn't. The volcano was about to spew. She couldn't let that happen. Not in here. And most of all, not in front of him.

Sheriff Behan leaned toward her and splayed his fingers across the table, his face obscured by the haze of smoke. "Listen now, don't go getting all het up. I'm sorry for your loss. I really am." He shook his head. "You'll need a place to stay." He jerked a thumb toward the saloon bar where the blowsy woman he'd been talking to earlier was filling glasses. "Miz Lydia can use a pretty little thing like you. Once you're cleaned up a bit…"

Grace pinned him with such a glare of hatred that his words faltered. She spat at his feet. "That's what I think of you. And your offer." Fists clenched at her sides, back ramrod straight, she spun and stormed out the door.

The sun blinded her as she banged outside. The wooden planks underfoot thrummed with the same hollowness that echoed in her chest.

To get out of the relentless sun beating down on her head, she unhitched Bullet and sidled into the shade of an alley across the street.

"They kick you out of the Bird Cage, honey?" The cowboy who'd accosted her in the bar swaggered across the street, now accompanied by a friend. "Maybe if you toned down your temper and cleaned up a bit, they'd take you back."

"Wash up, take off the dirty dress," his friend said eagerly.

"I ken help with that." The cowboy strode toward her, smacking the handle of his whip against his palm. His friend whooped and catcalled.

"Stay away from me," Grace said, low and menacing.

The cowboy threw up his hands and backed away a bit. "Ooo-wee, got a real tiger on my hands here. Maybe you need a bit of taming, eh?" He flicked his wrist as if to snap the whip.

Grace flinched.

He laughed, and the whip whistled through the air inches above Grace's head. Bullet let out a shrill whinny. He reared, tossing his mane, kicking out.

The cowboy leaped backward, lost his balance, and tumbled to the ground. He rolled away from the bucking horse. "Shoot that goldarned horse," he shouted. "It's crazy."

His crony yanked out a pistol and pointed it at Bullet.

"NO!" Grace's scream exploded from her, propelled by the agony of the past two days and shattering the noise around her into stillness. She threw her body in front of the horse. Not Bullet. She had nothing. No money. No food. No family. She'd die before she'd let them kill her only friend.

41

Passers-by stopped dead. All eyes fixed on Grace. Startled eyes. Curious eyes. Wary eyes. A few were sympathetic. Then Grace's gaze locked with one darker than her own, belonging to a swarthy young man. His hair, as dark as his eyes, lay loose against his tan deerskin tunic.

An Apache?

A shiver ran through Grace at the thought, but as she looked closer, a message seemed to flicker in his eyes that gave her courage.

The cowboy, still inching backward on his butt, shouted, "That danged horse nearly killed me! Shoot it!"

The man with the gun gave an impatient flick of his hand. "Outta the way, girlie. That horse is going down."

"Don't you *dare* touch my horse." Grace's words cracked through the air with greater emphasis than the whip. Bullet's hooves pawed the air above her head. He twisted in mid-air and crashed down beside her. Still quivering, his flanks heaving, Bullet snorted and nosed her. She ran her fingertips along his muzzle to quiet him.

The cowboy rose shakily to his feet and dusted off his chaps. "Get that girl outta the way."

Just as Grace remembered the revolver still tucked in her waistband, rough hands grabbed her and tried to drag her aside. She dug her heels into the dirt and refused to budge. The hands yanked harder, nearly pulling her off balance. Grace wriggled and clawed, and Bullet went wild. Striking out with his hooves, he emitted ear-piercing whinnies as the crowd surged around the scuffle.

"Stay back," Grace yelled, twisting away from her captors. "Give him some room."

Her gaze ranged across the crowd and came to rest on the sheriff, who stood in the doorway of the Bird Cage Theatre. Was he just going to stand there and watch? Her fury came to a boil and she channelled it as if into the narrow muzzle of a sawn-off shotgun, pointed in his direction. "You're a *coward*, Sheriff Behan." Her voice rang out across the hard-packed dirt street. "And if you won't track down those outlaws, I will. With or without your help."

The crowd stood in shocked silence. Then the swarthy young man nudged his horse past the still-frozen crowd. He wore knee-high moccasins and fringed leggings, but also a six-gallon hat. As she looked closer, Grace realized he wasn't Apache. His skin was a shade too light. His hair was too auburn. But before she could think about it more, the young man's eyes met hers again.

"You have quite some spirit, girl. Wish more hereabouts did." He glared at the sheriff, then tossed her a small buckskin pouch. "Use this for a meal, a bath." His voice was deep, but warm.

Then he turned to the men who had been taunting Grace. "You lay one hand on her or that horse, and I'll hunt you down." He stared at them until they slunk through the crowd.

Even the sheriff backed away from the door of the saloon.

But before Grace could say a word in protest or thanks, the rider wheeled his horse and galloped off toward the hills.

CHAPTER FOUR

Grace threaded her way through the crowd, her body pressed close to Bullet's quivering side to calm him. The palomino tossed his mane and snorted but didn't buck. Knots of people drew back as they passed, many casting wary looks at the horse and disapproving glances at her. Whispers whooshed past her like tumbleweed blowing in the hot desert air.

Grace straightened her spine and met everyone's stares boldly, but bitterness burned into her gut like lye. Not one of these staring strangers had come to her rescue.

And now that she had nowhere to stay, no family…? Grace blinked hard to stop her eyes from tearing up. No one would take her in, would they? Her family had no real friends in these parts. They'd been out on their own. Shoulders slumped, Grace leaned her head against Bullet's neck while fingering the pouch the stranger had given to her. At least someone had cared, but Grace didn't want charity. If she'd been thinking more quickly back there, she'd have thrown this back to him.

But now she had it and had no way to return it. She pulled the drawstring open and silver nuggets spilled into her palm. Her eyes widened, though she had no idea what they were worth. Pa had always bartered the horses for food and supplies. She'd heard of prospectors killing each other for silver, so it must be valuable – but the boy had said to get food and a bath, so maybe what he'd given her wasn't worth much?

Still, Grace didn't want to be beholden to anyone. She tipped her hand and poured the nuggets back into the pouch, sighing deeply. Exhaustion swept over her in a dizzying wave and hunger gnawed at her stomach. This pouch could buy her a meal and perhaps a place to sleep for the night. She had little choice unless she wanted to sleep in the street or out in the desert. And Bullet needed food and water. Grace clutched the lumpy pouch in her fist. She'd have to use the stranger's silver, but as soon as she could, she'd find out who he was and pay him back.

Down the street from the Bird Cage, Grace hitched Bullet to a post and entered a slightly more respectable-looking bordello. A woman, tightly corseted to emphasize the voluptuous curves spilling from her low-cut red and purple bodice, leaned one elbow on the counter and eyed Grace askance. "A little young for this bizness, ain't you?"

Through clenched teeth, Grace spat out each word. "I aim to pay for a room." She clinked the pouch against the wood and untied the rawhide string. Silver nuggets spilled onto the wood.

A greedy gleam shone in the woman's eyes. "Most share a room, but for this" – she slid predatory claws over the pile of silver – "I'll give you a room of your own. Private."

"My horse…?"

"Stable's included. Go around back to the alley. And you look like you could use some cleaning. For a bit more, I'll throw in a tub of hot water."

Grace shook the leather pouch. Empty.

"Too bad. Although…" The woman paused, her gaze skimmed Grace's body in the tight-fitting clothing. "You could pay for the bath in trade," she said with a smirk.

Grace couldn't keep the tremor of anger from her voice. "No, thank you."

A grizzled old man a few stools away slapped a coin onto the bar and stood. "Aw, Lil, lighten up. That poor girl's exhausted. Let her clean up and rest afore you coax her into the business. Seems to me she more than paid for a room in this joint." He settled his ten-gallon hat on his head, then tipped the brim in Grace's direction. "Don't let Lil cheat you. You deserve a meal and bath for what you paid. And a lot more." He raised a

47

warning eyebrow in Lil's direction.

Lil tossed her head back, setting the feather in her hair jiggling. She dropped the silver into the silken pouch she had strung about her waist. "Keep your nose outta my business, Tex." She turned to Grace. "You can use the tub my gals share. Down the hall from your room. Hot water's on the house."

Hands on hips, Tex continued staring at her, and Lil shot him an irritated look as she added grudgingly, "And dinner's included."

After caring for and stabling Bullet, Grace ate the tasteless meal Lil set before her. Then, trembling from exhaustion and suppressed emotions, she wended her way up the stairs to the bath, Pa's revolver concealed in the folds of her skirt.

A mousey girl, whose head drooped as if she'd endured one too many beatings, scuttled in with a steaming bucket to top up the greyish, well-used water in the hip bath. She handed Grace a sliver of soap.

Grace waited until the girl left, then removed the tintype from her bodice. Her family's faces stared up at her. Ma holding baby Abby. Pa, his hand resting on Daniel's shoulder. Grace standing between them. Zeke hadn't been born yet, but she'd never forget his face.

Pinching her lips together to smother a moan, Grace pressed the tintype to her heart. She stood, rocking back and forth, swallowing hard against the pain squeezing her chest. After a few minutes of agonizing memories, she pressed her lips to the picture and then set it and the gun on the chair in the corner of the room.

Slowly, she stripped off her smoke-tainted clothes, sank into the tepid water, and tried not to think of the others who had dirtied this bathwater before her. Ignoring the sting of the raw, oozing blisters on her hands, Grace scrubbed the soot and grime from her body and hair, wishing she could rub away the pain, the emptiness. Her skin reddened and grew tender, but Grace only scrubbed harder. The water cooled, but still Grace scrubbed. No matter how hard she scrubbed, though, she couldn't erase the memories that tumbled together in her mind – the cabin in ashes, the cross on the hillside.

As the night wore on, the patrons below became more and more raucous. Honky-tonk piano, fist fights, and shattering glass kept Grace tossing and turning. Laughing, seductive voices purred in the hallway outside her room accompanied by clomping boots and low growls. The sounds swirled around her, creating a kaleidoscope of images that punctuated her nightmares. Smoky gaslight from the sconces in the hallway flickered through the cracks in the beadboard walls, and the muted light and curls of smoke merged with memories of the flickering flames at the ranch. The stomp of Hale's boots. The jingle of spurs. The clink of a shovel.

Pounding startled Grace, and the jumbled dreams faded. She blinked at bright sunshine dazzling her. Why hadn't Pa shaken her awake at dawn? Why Ma hadn't started breakfast yet? Where was everyone? Cracks cobwebbed the yellowed plaster ceiling overhead. Plaster? Where was she? The cabin she called home had dark log beams.

Grace clutched the covers, fighting her way through the smoky haze of confusion. Soon numbness was creeping through her like a morning fog, chilling her, smothering her, as she remembered where she was. And why.

The doorknob rattled, shaking the chair she'd shoved underneath it for safety, and Grace jumped.

"You paying for another day? If not, get out. I got a bizness to run!"

"I'm leaving." The words came out choked, her throat hoarse, still clogged with sleep and unshed tears.

"Yer not outta there in a few minutes, the stable hand's gonna turn yer hoss loose," the voice outside the door growled. "Wild thing's been bucking up a storm."

Bullet. Grace snatched up her clothing that had dried stiff on the chair and dressed hurriedly. She stuffed the tintype in her bodice, grabbed Pa's gun, and raced for the stables.

As she rounded the corner and headed toward the alley, Grace could hear crashes, whinnies, and curses issuing from the stable. Two men screamed at each other above the clatter.

"That hoss should be shot!"

50

"Sheriff wouldn't like that. Wouldn't want that gal staying in town, stirring up trouble. Don't want her reminding people he's afeared of Hale."

"Afeared? Naw, he's living high off Hale's bribes."

No *wonder* the sheriff had ignored her. One hand gripping her gun and the other clenched into a fist, Grace sneaked along close to the stable wall, listening.

"If that's so," the deeper voice said, "why isn't Hale strutting around town? Rumour is he's hiding out in the Dragoon Mountains."

Grace's ears pricked at this. She'd seen the gang head out to the mountains – was it possible they were still out there?

"Hale will be back once the furore dies down," the other man retorted. "Right now Behan's covering for the Guiltless Gang. But if that new deputy finds out where Hale is, he'll put together a posse and go after them, cos word is this time that gang done killed a buncha kids too."

Not just any kids. Daniel and Abby and Zeke…

"Oh yeah…?"

Their tone was so dismissive that Grace's fury over Behan's cowardice – and everyone's acceptance of it – reached boiling point. She rushed toward the open stable door and stomped inside, her eyes flashing with anger. But with Bullet's hooves smashing against the stall door, the stable hands didn't even hear her enter.

"That little gal handled that horse; why can't you?" the

white-haired older man yelled with derision in his voice.

The younger one's hand slid to his holster. "Like I said, this horse oughta be shot—"

He stopped short as Grace pointed Pa's revolver at his back and pulled back the hammer. "You shoot my horse, I'll shoot you," she growled.

Both men turned and stared at her, wide-eyed.

The old man with grey stubble on his chin raised his hands as if in surrender, but a slow mocking grin spread across his face. He nudged the tall, skinny man beside him. "Best git the hoss for the *lady*." He drawled the last word, making it into an insult.

"I'll get Bullet myself." Grace strode toward the stall, keeping the gun pointed in their direction.

As soon as she reached him, Bullet quieted. He neighed and snorted as she unlatched and opened the stall, and then nudged her with his head, almost knocking the gun from her grasp. She saddled him up, checked the water pouch, and headed for the door.

When she passed them, the younger man backed away, but the older one grabbed for the saddlebag to stop her, making Bullet shy away. His voice menacing, he said, "If I was you, young lady, I'd get on outta Tombstone. I hear tell the gang's looking fer someone answering to your description. One that got away? Hate fer you to be the next victim."

"Yeah," the younger one joined in now, his words laced

with fake sympathy. "Wouldn't want you or that hoss shot. Accidents happen. Mistaken identity and all, you know."

Were they just trying to scare her, to pay her back because they hadn't liked being shown up by a girl? Or were she and Bullet really in danger?

She'd take no chances. Mounting Bullet quickly and giving the men one last disdainful stare, Grace dug in her heels and galloped away down the dusty streets. She had to get out of town. Away from the kind of men who wanted to shoot Bullet on sight. Away from a sheriff who was not only a coward, but crooked.

Away from her nightmares.

In the distance, the Dragoon Mountains rose, barren and rocky, dotted with patches of scrub and trees. Grief simmering and bubbling within her overflowed, threatening to consume her, but now Grace focused on one thought, one goal. If she could somehow track down Hale and flush him out of those mountains, the deputy could administer justice.

She and Bullet broke out into the open plains and were soon streaking across the desert. But although the freedom of the wide-open space felt a relief at first, within an hour the heat was scorching her, drenching her clothes in sweat and lathering Bullet's coat. The afternoon sun baked the clay and sand, sending waves of heat spiralling from the ground and puffs of dust clouding in the air behind them.

Against the clear blue sky the mountains had appeared

close, but hours later the granite peaks seemed no nearer. The landscape shimmered. Tufts of grass and small rocks wavered. Grace's eyes stung; her stomach cramped. *Water.* She'd been so anxious to get toward the mountains she'd been ignoring her growing thirst. She needed a drink and so did Bullet. She slid from the saddle and reached for the hide water bag – but it was flat. How could that be? She had filled it last night at the stable. Grace ran her hands along the sides and the bottom, trying to find the source of the leak. Was it an accident, or had one of the stable hands sabotaged it?

Grace slowed Bullet to a walk and headed for a lone cottonwood tree that trembled in and out of her vision, hoping desperately that it wasn't a mirage. Thirst was making her so tipsy she couldn't keep her balance. Soon her face was on fire and the inside of her mouth was dry and dusty. Too weak and woozy to remount, she staggered along beside Bullet with one hand on his neck to keep her balance, but after a few more steps Grace stumbled and fell. Bullet nudged her with his nose, but lethargy kept her pinned to the ground. She felt waves of acid rolling in her gut, cresting and splashing higher into her throat. Tight knots of pain twisted inside her belly. The sun was roasting her, draining every drop of energy from her body, every drop of moisture from her mouth.

She tried to say "I'm sorry" to Bullet, but her cracked, dried lips refused to even shape the words. Her eyelids drooped. They were heavy, so heavy…

She heard growls coming from her right. Through the haze closing around her, she could just make out grey bodies wavering in and out. Mexican wolves. Small and fierce. They usually preyed on cattle, trapping the weakest, but even in the fog of her brain Grace knew they wouldn't hesitate to attack her. She had to stand, get away before they tore out her throat, but she couldn't. She lay helpless, exposed, too weary to move as the wolves circled, closing in.

CHAPTER FIVE

Out of nowhere, a bullet skittered through the sand just past Grace's head. She flinched, unable to do anything more, but Bullet screamed and reared.

They've found me… The gang…

Pa's gun lay under the bunched folds of her skirt, but heaviness weighed her arm down. She just couldn't lift it.

Several more shots squeezed off in rapid succession. Why didn't they hit her? How many bullets would it take? But maybe death would be a welcome relief. She'd be with her family; she'd be at peace…

No!

If she died now, the Guiltless Gang would get away with

everything they had done.

She struggled, trying desperately to move. She heard a horse snort, and suddenly a low voice came from above her as she lay on the ground soothing Bullet. Grace struggled to open her eyes but her lids seemed to be glued shut. Did she want to see her killer? Surely he wouldn't miss from this close.

A shadow fell across her face and a figure leaned over her, blocking the relentless waves of heat. A hand slid under her head, tilting it up.

Did he plan to strangle her?

She should fight, but her arms flopped bonelessly like the limp arms of Abby's cornhusk doll. Grace finally managed to pry her eyes open to a squint, but blobs of swirling colour danced in front of her. Gradually, the brim of a black hat came into focus.

"P-Pa...?" Her parched lips could barely form the word. Reality came crashing back, and Grace shivered in spite of the broiling heat. She jerked as something brushed her mouth. Water. Precious drops of water. She gulped another mouthful and chased the drips with her tongue.

"Careful now," a deep voice said. "Drink slowly or you'll make yourself sick. Small sips."

The hand behind her head slid down to support her back and eased her into a sitting position. A hazy figure dressed in black blurred Grace's vision. A white band danced up and down on his neck. She struggled to focus, but eventually she could see a man smiling apologetically.

"I hope I didn't frighten you with those bullets. The noise scared off the wolves. They were probably only curious though. I don't believe they eat people but I didn't want to take a chance."

Spots whirled in front of Grace's eyes. She squeezed her eyes shut to stop the dizziness.

"When did you eat last?"

When *had* she eaten? The bordello…

"Yesterday." Her voice came out hoarse and whispery.

"I don't have much, but I'll share what I have." The man reached into the parfleche at his side and drew out a small ball of food. "It's pemmican. I buy it from the Indians."

He held it out, and Grace opened her mouth like a baby bird, helpless, her arms limp at her sides.

He broke off a piece and fed it to her.

Grace chewed slowly, savouring the tart dried berries, bits of beef jerky, and melting fat. The raging acid in her stomach began to calm.

The stranger gave Bullet some water, then knelt beside her again. "Now let's get you into the shade. Think you can stand?"

Her arms and legs wouldn't cooperate, so he picked her up and carried her to the cottonwood tree she'd been heading toward before she collapsed. He settled her under the low-hanging branches, and the air felt several degrees cooler.

"Who are—" She croaked out the words.

"John Byington, at your service."

John Byington? The name sounded familiar, but Grace's mind was so addled she couldn't recall where she'd heard it before.

"The Good Lord must have directed me this way today. What are you doing way out here?"

What *was* she doing out here? Why had she come? A thick cloud obscured her thoughts.

"Are you a runaway?"

Grace shook her head. Her tongue was still too thick in her mouth to answer.

John Byington lifted a thick black book from his bag. A Bible.

Now Grace knew who he was. The saddlebag preacher. Ma always insisted they ride into town when he came through once a month to preach. That white band at his neck was a clerical collar.

Clutching the Bible in one hand, Reverend Byington knelt beside her and took her hand. "Why don't we pray? Thank God that He spared your life?"

"Spared *my* life?" The words barely trickled out, as if her throat were an unprimed pump. "Wh-what about my family?"

Then the rusty tap opened, and tears gushed out along with her words. Byington held her hand while Grace spilled the whole story of what had happened at her home, concern etching a frown into his forehead. After she finished, he remained silent for a long time, his eyes filled with empathy. Finally, he cleared his throat. "I'm mighty sorry you've been through so much pain." His voice sounded husky, as though he were holding back tears himself. "But God spared you – twice. He must have a special purpose for your life—"

"The only purpose I have in life is to see those killers brought to justice," Grace spat. "God has nothing to do with it." The fog in her brain was clearing, leaving her with a terrible headache.

The Reverend sighed. "I don't blame you for being bitter, child. But the hostility in your heart will poison you more than those you hate." He let go of her hand, opened his Bible, and thumbed through the pages. "The Good Book says, '*For if you forgive men when they sin against you, your Heavenly Father will also forgive you. But if you do not forgive men their sins, your Father will not forgive your sins.*'"

"*My* sins? What about theirs?" Pent-up fury choked Grace's words.

"It is not for you to judge. Leave justice up to God."

"How can I trust God? Was killing my family His idea of justice?" The sun shimmering on the rocks made her eyes sting and increased the pounding in her head.

The creases in Reverend Byington's weather-beaten face deepened. "No one knows God's plans or purposes. And though it may not seem like it, He loves you and cares about you."

Grace sucked in a sharp breath that seemed to pierce through her shattered heart. "I used to believe that until … until…" She pinched her lips together to stop them from trembling. When she spoke again, she made her words short and sharp, to hide the hollowness inside. "I don't need God's love. Or anyone else's. Love only leads to heartache. Do you know what it feels like to see everyone you've ever loved…" She closed her eyes, fought off the visions of the cross on the hill. Her voice when it came was shaky and filled with all the pain welling up inside. "I'll never love anyone *ever* again."

"My dear, that's your pain speaking. I'll pray that, in time, God will soften your heart." He held out a hand to help Grace to her feet. "Let's head back to town. I'll see that you get a proper meal, and I believe I know someone who might be able to take you in."

His kindness in spite of her outburst brought tears to Grace's eyes. "Thank you for the offer. But I have a mission."

The look the preacher gave her – part pity, part judgement – made Grace squirm. But she wouldn't give up until she'd brought every last one of that gang to justice.

"I can't leave a young girl wandering the desert alone," he insisted. "If I hadn't come along, you would have died."

"Perhaps that would have been for the best."

Reverend Byington frowned. "Untimely deaths are never good." He softened his sharp tone. "As you well know."

She hung her head and scuffed her boot on the ground.

"No, they're not."

"And despite what you think of God at this moment, He has a special plan for your life…"

Grace bit her tongue to keep from arguing and kept her eyes averted so he couldn't read defiance in them.

When she didn't answer, the preacher laid a hand on her shoulder. "Things may look different once you've had some rest and more food. Are you still dizzy? If so, I can walk beside your horse instead of riding."

"I'm *not* going back to town." She knew if she told him exactly what she planned, he wouldn't let her go. But Grace intended to track down those criminals. If she had to, she'd lead the deputy and posse back to their lair herself.

"Well, you can't stay out *here*, child." The preacher rubbed his chin. "If you won't come back to town, then the Joneses have a ranch just east of here. They'd be glad to take you on if you're willing to work." He squinted up at the sun. "You can probably make it there with your horse within the hour. Head due east on that trail there. If you're sure you're all right to go it on your own."

"I-I am. Thank you," Grace murmured but kept her gaze on the ground. She appreciated his thoughtfulness, all the more so after the way the people in town had treated her. She couldn't tell him she had no intention of heading that way.

"They'll be pleased to have you. Martha's been ill for a while now, and taking care of six children has just about done her in. I'm sure she'd be glad of an extra hand. They have horses too." He pulled at his lower lip and looked thoughtful. "Not sure they'd let a young girl help with their horses, but they'd stable yours. You'd have a roof over your head. And both John and Martha are fine Christians, raising their children to love the Good Book." He smiled as he tucked his Bible into his saddlebag. "And I'm sure they'll talk you out of this darkness in your heart."

"Perhaps, sir." She couldn't say anything more.

"You had better take this." Reverend Byington handed her his water pouch.

"But you'll need it, won't you?"

"Not as much as you do." He also held out his leather bag. "I'm afraid there's not much pemmican left, but you can use this to store your things." He pointed to the gun and the tintype.

Grace was overwhelmed by his kindness. "But I… How can I repay you?"

"You owe me nothing. Show your gratitude to God by forgiving those who have wronged you."

Grace pursed her lips to keep the words from bursting out. *Those criminals? Never.*

He looked at her dubiously. "Perhaps I *should* accompany you…"

"No, no. I'll be fine." She had to get away before he dragged her to the Joneses. "Uh, didn't you say someone was waiting

63

for you in town?"

"Yes, but he'll understand that I must be about the Lord's business."

"Well, as you said, it's not far to the ranch, right?" She had to convince him to head to town so she could get on with her plans.

His eyes still held reluctance, but he sighed. "Yes. And remember, the Joneses are good people. I'll be out this way after the Sunday sermon, so I can check on you."

"OK. OK – thank you," Grace said hastily.

As soon as he bid her good day, she rode off in the direction he'd indicated, waiting until the granite outcrops near the foot of the mountains hid her and Bullet. Then she turned and headed straight up the mountain.

After hours of climbing, Grace stopped for a rest. Hadn't the preacher mentioned he'd filled his water pouch at a stream in this direction? Or had she gotten turned around when she'd pretended to ride toward the ranch? She pulled Bullet to a halt and dismounted, then opened the pouch the preacher gave her to nibble on some more of the pemmican.

As she chewed, she realized something. Pa's pistol was in the pouch – but where was the tintype? She took out the rest of the pemmican, the gun, turned the bag upside down and shook it. She felt around inside for holes or a lining. No! She couldn't have lost it. Grace stood up, searched all around the rocky ground. She'd slid the tintype into the pouch. She knew she had. Where could it have fallen out?

Grace backtracked, panic rising in her chest, trying to remember the twists and turns she'd taken, but to no avail. She searched until the sun was starting to set, but couldn't find the tree the preacher had settled her under.

Her heart sinking, she realized that she and Bullet needed to find more water so they wouldn't run out again. She couldn't keep searching. The tintype was gone. A tear trickled down her cheek, followed by another. She'd lost the last tie to her family, her last memento of a happier time. Greyness settled over her mind like ashes from the burned-out cabin, blanketing her in gloom, and she squinted despondently at the setting sun. She needed to get up into the Dragoon Mountains to discover where Hale and his gang were hiding out, so she could lead the deputy to them. But night was falling, and she knew she couldn't stay out in the open unprotected.

She pulled on the reins to turn Bullet uphill, and with each step away from the place where the tintype might lie, Grace's heart grew heavier and a ball of hardness settled in her chest. And she *had* to keep pulling her mind back to one thought – her mission. If she started grieving, she'd never stop. Giving in to sadness would paralyse her.

"Bullet," she whispered. "You're all I have left." She loosened her grip on the reins and let the horse have his head. He walked slowly, nose down. She'd never forgive herself if he collapsed. More water first. Then Hale.

65

Bullet took them higher into the granite prison, and endless piles of rocks and sharp, steep cliffs began to rise all around them. The going was rough, and several times the horse stumbled when loose rocks slid under his feet, but he plodded on. They mounted another ridge, and in the growing dusk she could make out a clump of trees to the right.

Trees? Maybe they'd find water there. Grace didn't even need to touch the lead rope. As if drawn in that direction, Bullet headed straight toward them.

Grace heard it before she saw it, and she sighed with relief — water trickling over rocks. A welcome, wonderful sound. Bullet's tired gait changed. He lifted his drooping head and pranced forward. They plunged through a thicket and emerged by a stream.

She slid from Bullet's back and let him wade into the water. If she'd found a stream out here in the desert where water was so scarce, Hale had to be around her somewhere too. He and his men couldn't survive without water. If she followed the stream upward, surely she'd come upon their hideout soon enough. But she'd have to be cautious and find the Guiltless Gang before they spotted her.

First she drank, then she splashed cold water on her face and hands to wash away the grime and dust. Grace longed to wade in beside Bullet, but darkness was fast descending. Nights in the desert grew cold this time of year, and the night air in the mountains had already turned nippy. She needed a place to sleep, somewhere with shelter, where she could stay warm and dry. While Bullet nibbled the grasses along the bank, Grace searched the steep cliffs for an overhang, somewhere they'd be safe.

The moon was rising now – a small sliver – and pinpricks of stars sparkled in the night sky. Grace had often sat on the porch with her parents after the others were in bed, gazing out at them. Enjoying the beauty of the night, listening to coyotes' distant, mournful howl.

Here, the coyotes sounded much closer though – dangerously so. Grace shivered. Mountain lions. Mexican wolves. Bobcats. Many wild animals made their homes here in the hills. And out here she had no cabin walls to hide inside. No Pa with a shotgun across his knees. No protection other than his Colt pistol. Grace patted the leather bag the preacher had given her, her hands resting on the bulge of the gun. At least she hadn't lost that. Pa had taught her to shoot, but she hadn't used a gun other than for an occasional rattler. Her skills were rusty. She hoped she wouldn't need to use it.

While Bullet ate, Grace continued to study the nearby cliffs. She could see several promising overhangs and darker indentations that might hold caves. When Bullet had had his fill, Grace mounted and headed up the steep trail. Pa had taught her to watch for signs of wild animals, but unlike the sands near the ranch, where even sidewinders' bodies left trails, the rocky ground here didn't seem to hold tracks, so she searched for scat. Though she spotted scattered piles, most of the animal droppings looked dried, so maybe she would be OK here.

She spotted an overhang, low and narrow but she could just about crawl under it. She'd been up in these mountains a few times with Pa, so she knew that sometimes it snowed this time of year – a brief powdery shower that usually melted soon after sunrise. Under this overhang she'd be protected from snow or from the rare thunderstorms that sent floods crashing into the arroyos. Yes, this would do.

Pulling Bullet to a halt, Grace dismounted. No scat outside. She knelt and peered inside. Dusk made it difficult to see much, but cobwebs crisscrossed the opening, so it obviously hadn't been used in awhile. With a dead branch, she scraped out the webs and bits of debris. Then, too tired to gather wood for a fire, she snaked her way underneath and curled up on the rocky ground, wishing Bullet could fit inside too. The warmth of his body might ward off some of the loneliness of gazing at the distant stars. She rubbed her arms to relieve the chill that raised goose flesh on her arms, but the slight warmth from the friction didn't ease the iciness that froze her from the inside out. Unfamiliar rustlings, howls, and hoots kept her awake most of the night, until finally exhaustion overtook her.

*   *   *

The sun had not yet risen when Bullet whinnied, waking Grace. Her sleep had been restless and the cold dampness of the stones had seeped into her bones. She felt bruised from head to toe after spending the night on the hard ground, and she shivered uncontrollably in the pre-dawn air.

After checking to be sure the gun was in the pouch, Grace snugged it like a saddlebag to Bullet. Sadness filled her as she remembered the lost tintype. Should she search for it again? No. Much as her heart ached, she had to push on. Find out where Hale and his gang were hiding; get the deputy and a posse. Then she would retrace her route from town.

In the dawn's greyness, Grace walked Bullet down to the creek. Most of the forest sounds had stilled, and the silence felt eerie, pressing in around her. The clip-clop of Bullet's hooves on the rocks echoed noisily.

A cloudy mist rose from the creek, and through the trees ahead Grace could make out vague shapes. The gang? She stopped, her heart quickening until she realized it was just a writhing mass of animals, all drinking in the stream. Shapes moved, separated. They lifted their heads, suddenly alert at her arrival. Grace just made out the rounded horns of pronghorn deer before they charged off into the trees. She drank some water and then refilled the water container. Bullet had wandered farther down the bank, nibbling the grasses. Grace stood and stretched…

But she stopped dead, hands still in the air, as a vague,

misty shape emerged from the gloom. Not quite as high in the back as a horse, and broader and bulkier through the body. The creature lifted its head to show small rounded ears, a pointy snout.

A bear.

It sniffed the air and looked straight at Grace.

Their eyes locked, and it started lumbering toward her.

CHAPTER SIX

Run! Grace's inner voice screamed but her muscles went rigid, immobilizing her.

Bullet whinnied in alarm but Grace couldn't tear her gaze from the bear.

Her father's warning ran through her head. As if Pa stood behind her, his hand on her shoulder, his words sounded clearly in Grace's head: *Never run from a bear.*

"Pa?" she whispered.

His presence surrounded her. It almost seemed that if she reached out her hand, she could touch him. But she knew she was alone, and panic clouded her mind. Pa had taught her a rhyme about bears. What was it?

The bear lumbered closer.

Grace's throat closed. If she backed away slowly, would it attack?

The gun. Why hadn't she kept the gun with her? Pa had never gone anywhere without this gun.

The rhyme. Think of the rhyme. How did it start? Grizzly...

Grizzly, grizzly, play dead. Black bear, black bear, hit it in the head.

But which kind of bear was it? Grace couldn't tell – in the gloom its coat looked as grey as the sky. The hump on the back of its neck rippled with each step and its white teeth gleamed in the low dawn light. And those eyes. They pinned her in place.

If she chose wrong, she'd be dead.

Pa's voice came again. *Make noise. Try to scare it off.*

Grace cleared her throat, but her spit had dried in her mouth. All that came out was a choking sound.

Do it, Grace. Try again.

I'm trying, Pa. Grace swallowed hard. She tried to wet the inside of her mouth, loosen her tongue. She opened her mouth and a weak gurgle came out.

Again. Try again, Pa's voice commanded.

A shrill scream came from her lips this time, growing louder, stronger. She clapped her hands, stomped her feet in a crazy frenzied dance, and finally the bear stopped for a moment. Grace couldn't tear her gaze from its eyes – they seemed to glow: yellow, piercing.

Then the bear advanced once more. Her stomach flipped over.

Grace bent, scrabbling blindly on the ground for loose rocks until finally her hand closed over a large chunk. She stood and hurled it without hesitating.

Bullseye.

The bear shook its head and growled deep in its chest.

Grace scooped more up handfuls of rocks and sticks and tossed them furiously. With yowls of pain, the bear crouched, but it didn't leave. Instead, it sprang straight toward her.

With a loud squeal, Bullet charged. Bear and horse met in a snapping, snarling mass of tearing teeth, flying hooves, slashing claws, growls, whinnies – and screams.

Grace's was the loudest.

"No, Bullet!"

Blood dripped from his flank. *No, no, no.*

Grace launched herself at the bear from the side and pounded a rock against its skull. Jaws wide, it tipped its head sideways, aiming for her neck. Just as it did, Bullet reared. Blood streaming down his legs, he crashed down onto the bear's back, rescuing her – but the beast's claws slashed out, raking down Grace's arm and tearing her flesh.

The bear rolled sideways, whimpering.

Grace took the opportunity and raced toward Bullet to get to the saddlebag. She caught up with him as he bucked and reared, and fumbled in the leather pouch for the gun. She'd never let it leave her side from now on. But before she could pull the pistol out, the bear stumbled to its feet and shook himself.

She stared at it, panting hard. What was it going to do?

The huge creature let out a single, bone-shaking growl … then turned and crashed through the woods. Grace exhaled sharply and turned back to Bullet. Afraid to mount the horse with his body bleeding so badly, Grace grabbed the reins and quickly led him away, making sure to stay close to the stream. Panic built in her chest and her breath came in short, sharp gasps. Bullet kept pace beside her but his own breathing was wheezy and whistling. They had to stop and rest. Her whole ribcage seemed to ache from the thumping of her heart.

When Grace thought they were far enough from the bear, she halted, one hand wrapped around the gun. She studied the area around her for any signs of wildlife, wary of another possible attack. But other than skittering ground squirrels and chirping birds, the area seemed deserted.

A sudden searing sting drew Grace's attention to her arm. There were slash marks that ran from wrist to elbow, and her eyes widened in shock at the blood that flowed warm and wet from the torn skin of her inner arm. How had she not felt this until now?

"Oh… Oh my Lord…"

Now the pain rushing through her made her head spin.

74

Shaking uncontrollably, Grace sank to the ground and set the gun beside her. She wrapped her hand around the wound, trying to hold it closed, to staunch the bleeding, but blood soon coated her fingers.

"Got to … stop it…" she whispered to herself.

Using her good arm, she lifted the hem of her dress to her mouth. Clamping the fabric between her teeth, she tore off a strip, then she sat on the ground and cradled her arm in her lap. She looped a makeshift bandage around her forearm and pulled it tight with her teeth.

Beside her, Bullet snorted. *Oh, no.* Two of his legs and his flank were a bloodied mess.

Bullet. She had to take care of him.

Grace forced herself to her feet. Dizzy and shaky, she led Bullet to the water and tried to wash off the blood. The water stung her injured arm so badly it was all she could do to keep from passing out. The water swirling around them turned pinkish, making her stomach roil.

When she'd washed away as much of the blood as she could, she nudged Bullet back to the grassy bank and collapsed beside him. Stuffing her sopping-wet skirt into her mouth, Grace bit down on the damp material, but now that it was wet it wouldn't tear the way the dry fabric had. Frantically, Grace chewed and pulled at it a bit at a time until finally she'd managed to make several strips.

"I'm so sorry" she whispered as she wrapped the pieces

around the mangled flesh of Bullet's legs and pressed a wad of fabric to the wound on his flank. Holding her injured arm close to her chest, she reached for Bullet's reins. They had to get out of here. Did enraged bears return? Grace didn't know. All she knew was that they ought to get out of here fast.

Bullet hobbled along at her side, and with her good arm Grace shoved aside underbrush, hugging her injured arm close to her side. Blood had already soaked through the cotton she'd tied around it, and the bandages on Bullet's legs were reddening too. His gait grew stiffer as the sun the rose high in the sky.

Hunger clawed at Grace's belly. She had finished the last of the preacher's pemmican last night and had had nothing to eat since. She looked around her desperately, but the brush and trees had thinned, so there was nothing that looked even a little edible – but frogs splashed in the water nearby, and silvery fish darted past.

If only I could catch one of those…

If Pa were here, he'd know what to do. She thought hard. Ma had once told her that Indians used spears for fishing. Would a long stick work instead? Grace searched for a one with a sharp point, but most of the branches nearby were too thick, too brittle, or too willowy. Finally, she found a sturdy stick with a slightly pointed end and quickly sawed the branch against the rough bark of a tree to sharpen it as much as possible. Then Grace waded into the water a little way and settled, standing still so she could see the fish as they swam by, but they seemed to dart away before the stick even descended. Her arm soon ached from thrusting her homemade spear down again and again.

She was faint from hunger and getting dizzier by the minute. If she didn't eat something soon, she'd collapse. If she had a net, she could stretch it between the rocks … but how could she make a net? Her skirt might have worked, but most of it had been shredded for bandages. Still, she used her teeth and her good arm to tear off the remaining swathe, completely exposing her buckskin breeches with their shredded knees.

After stretching the fabric between two rocks, Grace weighed down the two lower edges with heavy stones. At first the fish avoided the opening and swam past the rock on the other side. Was her shadow scaring them off? Or was it the floating fabric?

Grace forced herself to stay motionless, to become one with the rocks and the stream. Her back cramped but she remained in position, hunched over, clenching the top ends of the fabric. Her arm, now bleeding profusely from the exertion, sent sparks of pain shooting through the left half of her body – but finally one fish broke off from the school and headed between the rocks.

With one quick motion, Grace scooped the fabric around the slippery, wriggling fish. She almost lost it, but at last, with all four corners gathered, she held the dripping, thrashing bundle away from her body and stumbled up the bank. She needed to start a fire.

"I *think* I know how Pa did this…" she said to herself.

She laid the fish on the ground and gathered a pile of dried grass and broken twigs, then found a piece of sagebrush with a point on one end, and a branch that had split partway open. After inserting the point into the opening, she twirled the sagebrush between her hands. Pa always made this look so easy. He'd twirled one stick against the other, and before you knew it he'd caused enough friction for smoke to start forming in tendrils. Then he'd add the dried buffalo grass until *whoosh* – it caught.

But she had no such luck. After what felt like hours, Grace gave up. Her fingers were stiff and cramped, and her drenched bandage did almost nothing now to staunch the flow of blood. The fish had long ago stopped flopping. She stared at it. Could she eat it uncooked? *Ugh.* But if animals ate raw fish, she could too, couldn't she?

Using a sharp stone, she scraped off the scales and split it open. Then she closed her eyes and lifted the fish to her lips. She could barely choke down the rubbery, slimy flesh, but hunger pangs urged her on. When she'd eaten as much as she could stomach, she wrapped the rest in the fabric and called to Bullet. They needed to move ahead if they were to have any hope of finding Hale and his gang.

* * *

Hours of plodding uphill, Bullet hobbling beside her, were followed by another night of restless sleep, punctuated by nightmares. Grace huddled under a pile of dirt and leaves to ward off the frigid night air, and woke to another day of raw stinking fish. It being all she had to eat, she resorted to sucking desperately on its bones. Both her and Bullet's bandages stuck to their own dried blood, and Grace cradled her throbbing arm close to her body as they trudged through undergrowth and stumbled over stones. Sipping water silenced her constant hunger pangs only temporarily.

But through it all, one thing stayed constant – Pa's gun clutched in her hand.

Then they mounted another hill, and suddenly Grace cried out in relief. There before her were several bushes filled with purple berries. They looked like the berries that were in the preacher's pemmican, except these were round and plump, and the ones in the pemmican were dried. Her heart dancing, Grace staggered toward them, scattering several birds pecking on the fruit. She feasted, popping berry after berry into her mouth, then finally tore herself away to the nearby stream to rinse the stinking fabric fish net with her good arm, keeping the gun beside her on the bank. Rushing back to the bushes, she spread the cloth on the ground and filled it with as many berries as she could.

A full stomach gave her renewed energy. She whistled for Bullet, and he plodded toward her. *Poor boy*. His gait had grown slower and more unsteady. Fear gripped Grace as he hobbled closer. His legs were so swollen under the bandages that the fabric edges had made indentations in his skin. She squatted to unwind the strips, but they were stuck. She'd have to soak them off when they stopped for the night.

But a few hours later, it was Grace who was in trouble. She felt sudden, stabbing pains shooting through her belly, leaving her gasping for breath, and clutched her stomach as it churned horribly, nausea rising in waves, her oesophagus burning. Had the raw fish made her sick? Grace tried to press on further, but the cramps doubled her over and she slid to the ground.

Shivers wracked her body. Her teeth were chattering but her body was burning up. Sweat dripped down her face and stung her eyes. *Water*. She needed water. Grace tried crawling toward the nearby stream, but her throbbing arm refused to support her weight. Her forearm had swollen inside the bandage, just like Bullet's wounds, and the skin above it was now purplish red. But Grace was too weak to loosen the bandage. She collapsed a few feet from the stream bed, her body spasming with dry heaves.

The gun. She still clutched the gun. Bullet stood over her, his shadow blocking the sun, blocking her view of the buzzards circling overhead. The palomino's shadow grew, floated past her eyes, turned into the mocking shapes of Hale and his men. They pointed guns at her. Hale opened his mouth. It yawned like an open grave. A bear leaped from the darkness. Grace screamed. Her body jerked…

As if from a distance, she heard Bullet neighing, and the nearby brush parted. Had Hale's men found her? Grace was shivering too violently to get to her feet. She couldn't even lift the gun. Desperation and sorrow flooded her eyes.

A cool hand descended on her forehead, followed by water. Icy cold drips slid down her temples and onto her neck. Grace flinched, and her muscles convulsed. She rolled onto her side and retched. Hands gripped her shoulders, supporting her until her stomach emptied.

Weak and spent, Grace lay panting and the strange hands let go of her. Moments later, more water trickled down her face. A wet cloth pressed against her forehead, slid down over her eyes, swiped across her face. Blessed coolness, but Grace couldn't stop shaking.

"P-preacher?" she croaked. Had he followed her?

A deep chuckle rumbled beside her. "First time I was ever accused of that."

"Who … are you?" Grace croaked. She opened her eyes, trying to focus, but the sun burned her eyes and left the face above her in shadow. Grace had a vague impression of the brim of a Stetson dipping toward her, long dark hair falling forward, and even through her fever she realized she recognized the figure.

"You. Again." The boy who'd thrown her the pouch of silver.

"Yes, me again. What are you doing way out here? You didn't have enough trouble in town?"

If she could catch the wisps of thoughts floating in her brain, she'd answer him. But she couldn't remember how she'd ended up here. Only two words were emblazoned in her memory.

"Elijah Hale," she whispered.

"Are you *crazy*? You came out here chasing an outlaw? A girl? Alone?"

More convulsions shook her and she couldn't respond.

He glanced from her purple-stained fingers to the cloth she'd dropped. "You didn't eat those berries, did you?"

Grace tried to nod but it set off more spasms. She rolled onto her side, choking. He held her shoulders again while she emptied her stomach. Then he wiped her face and mouth with the wet cloth.

He shook his head. "Any fool knows pokeberries are poisonous."

Grace tried to protest that those berries looked like the ones in the preacher's pemmican but he didn't give her a chance.

"You could have died out here if I hadn't come along." He leaned over her, frowning. "And I had to rescue you that day in town too."

"Are you … following me?"

"Of course not."

"First in town. Now here." Through her fogged brain, Grace

82

remembered the silver. She had to tell him she'd pay him back.

"I have more important things to do," he said. "But I'm not surprised I ended up saving your neck again."

She frowned. "You … you…" But before she could choke out any more words, blackness closed over her mind and everything went dark.

CHAPTER SEVEN

In the distance, Grace was aware of stomping, chanting, jingling bells. Pounding drums vibrated the air, and feet slapped the earth around her, jarring her body. Her head thumped and ached.

The noise faded. Shivers wracked her body. She was burning and freezing at the same time. Cool hands touched her forehead. Liquids dribbled between her chattering teeth and down her throat. Grace struggled to open her eyes but her eyelids were much too heavy.

Smoke swirled around her, filling her lungs and making her choke. Grace thrashed. She had to get out. To save Zeke. She reached out to cradle him close to her chest, but pain ripped through her arm, jerking her awake.

Where was she?

Poles arched overhead, baskets dangled from the rafters. Through the haze Grace made out walls that looked like tufts of grass.

Fur lined the hard ground under her. A rough wool blanket covered her.

A strange murmuring sound came from above, and a dark-skinned man leaned over her, a cotton headband wrapped around his forehead. His long black hair fell forward to almost brush her chest.

Grace sucked back a scream and squeezed her eyes shut.

An Apache.

She'd been captured by the Apache? Would they torture her? Scalp her?

Did they kill you first and then take your scalp? Or did they do it while you were still alive? Was he getting ready to kill her?

Grace watched him through slitted eyelids. What was that in his hand? He chanted strange words and shook what looked like a gigantic leather baby rattle painted with yellow and blue designs. Eagle feathers dangled from the handle. Was it a club?

He bent closer, laid a hand on her forehead. She flinched, and her chest constricted so she could barely breathe. She swallowed, trying to suck back the terror. A scream gurgled up from her chest and she reared back. She had to get away—

"You are awake. That is good."

He spoke English? Grace opened one eye, then the other. That strange rattle had disappeared. In its place, he held a handful of eagle feathers. With a brushing motion, he spread the smoke, and another cloud drifted toward her. Grace coughed, and tears rolled down her cheeks.

"You hurt here?" He tapped his fingers to his forehead, making the shell necklaces on his buckskin-covered chest clink together.

Was he warning her he was going to hurt her? Or was he asking if she had a headache?

His broad smile seemed friendly enough, but Grace's body stayed on high alert. She searched for an exit. Behind him, a buffalo hide hung across a doorway. If her exhausted muscles would cooperate, maybe she could distract him and run. She tried to scoot back when he turned to pick up a gourd bowl behind him, but her left arm throbbed so much it couldn't support her weight.

The man turned around again, bowl in hand, and pointed to his chest. "I am Cheveyo."

Was that his name? He wouldn't introduce himself before he scalped her, would he? Grace's heartbeat slowed from a gallop to a canter.

"My people call me Spirit Warrior." Then he pointed to her. "You?"

"Me?" Her voice squeaked. "You mean my name?"

He nodded.

"I'm Grace."

"Gurrr-asss," he repeated. "English is hard to speak. Ahote teaches me, but I do not always learn well."

"How … how did I get here?"

"Ahote find you. He brought you here."

"Ahote knows English?"

Cheveyo's brow crinkled, then he said, "He is English."

Did he mean Ahote was English or that he spoke English? If Ahote was English, maybe he could help her escape. At least, she hoped he could. Grace tried to make her next question casual. "Is Ahote here?"

"He is hunting."

"When will he return?" *Soon. Please let it be soon.* She had to get away from here. She had to carry on, to track down the Guiltless Gang…

"If hunt goes well, he will be back soon. But in your language…" Cheveyo stared at the ceiling, his face scrunched up as if he were thinking. After a few seconds, he looked at Grace again. "Ahote means 'Restless One'. So maybe he will return soon … maybe not." He smiled.

So she was trapped here until this Restless One returned? And if he did, would he even help her escape? She couldn't wait for him – she had to find her own way out. Would the Apache leave her alone, unguarded, though? Cheveyo had to sleep sometime… But she'd need Bullet.

Bullet! How had she forgotten about him? "My horse!"

87

Grace said, her voice rising in urgency. "Where is my horse?"

Cheveyo looked grave and shook his head.

Was Bullet dead? No, no, it couldn't be...

"Your horse needs much time to heal, like you." Cheveyo leaned forward and lifted Grace's arm gently. "That needs more medicine."

She stared at her own limb, shocked. Red and tender, her arm had swollen to twice its normal size. In place of the makeshift bandage, a white cloth soaked in something had been wrapped around it.

Cheveyo walked over to a stone bowl and pestle. He crushed bits of bark, poured in some water from a container over the fire, and brought the mash over to her.

"What it that?" She grimaced, looking at it.

"White willow bark. It will take away pain and swelling."

After unwinding the bandage, Cheveyo applied the warm paste to Grace's arm. Then he rewrapped it with a clean bandage and soon the pulsing ache in her arm was soothed.

From containers lining the wall, Cheveyo mixed some herbs into the remaining willow bark. He poured the herbs into a gourd bowl and diluted it with more hot water. Then he knelt beside her with the steaming concoction. He slid one hand behind her back, propped her up, and brought the gourd bowl to her lips. "This will make you strong and well."

Grace turned her head away. He wanted her to drink the same stuff he put on her arm? What if it were poison – or a sleeping potion? Who knew what the Apache had planned for her. She choked as another cloud of smoke drifted into her nostrils. Liquid sloshed out of the bowl and splashed on the earthen floor. In one swift motion, Cheveyo set the bowl on the ground, leaned her forward, and patted her on the back until she got her breath back.

Grace's eyes watered, and she kept hacking. "That smoke..." She waved her good arm toward the foggy room and forced herself to keep coughing. "I need air." Maybe she could convince him to take her outside. "Air," she repeated, and followed it with gasping noises.

Cheveyo continued to pat her back.

"Outside." She tried to sound like she was about to collapse.

"Smoke is good." He waved more smoke her way. "Smudging. It will help you heal. The sacred plants have great power to cleanse."

Grace obviously wouldn't get out of this hut that way. She needed another plan.

Cheveyo picked up the bowl again. "This is good for fever."

Grace stared at it suspiciously.

"You are afraid to taste it?" Cheveyo tipped the gourd to his own lips and took a sip. "It will not hurt you."

Warily, Grace sipped the bitter tea he held out.

Cheveyo studied her with compassionate eyes. He motioned to the gourd bowl. "That will heal your body, but you must heal here too." He tapped his forehead.

What did he know about her state of mind? Perhaps it would never heal. But bringing Hale and the Guiltless Gang to justice might give her at least a *chance* of mending it. She had wasted too much time already. Grace set down the bowl and pushed back the blanket.

"Please. *I must go*."

But when she tried to move away from his supporting hands, her whole body went limp. Cheveyo shook his head. "You are not ready."

Grace couldn't let that gang get away. How long would they stay holed up in the mountains? They could be gone already for all she knew. She had to get after them.

"Revenge is not the way of the spirit. You must also heal here." He laid a hand over his heart. "*This* is the great healer. It can make you sick. It can make you well. But only *you* can choose to let go of what makes you ill inside."

Grace let out a tight, dismissive laugh. "I'm *ill* because I ate pokeberries and was gored by a bear…"

"Yes, this is true. But you also hold much hurt and anger here." Again Cheveyo thumped his chest. "Only if you let it go, will you heal."

"I only hold a need for justice." And Grace knew she would never let that go. Never. Not until every last one of the Guiltless Gang was jailed or hanged.

Cheveyo shook his head. "Let Usen mete out justice."

"Who is Usen?" Grace said eagerly. Would he help her

find the gang?

Cheveyo pointed toward the sky. "Usen is the Great Creator. It is his place to say what should happen. He makes all things right."

Grace sighed deeply. No one and no *thing* could make this right. And why did everyone she ran into believe God was the source of justice? Perhaps before everything that had happened to her she would have said the same … but now? Didn't they see all the terrible things in the world? How could anyone trust in a God like that? And as for letting God mete out *justice*?

She'd seen that first-hand, and she wanted no part of it. Just as she'd seen the sheriff's brand of justice. The only justice she wanted right now was what she could get herself. She couldn't depend on people or on the law or on God. She was alone in her fight for true justice.

"Peace in the heart puts the body in harmony with the universe, and all that is," Cheveyo said softly. He lifted the buffalo skin that covered the door and stepped outside. "To walk in happiness, let the hurt go…"

Now he sounded like Reverend Byington. In spite of what Cheveyo and the preacher said, Grace wouldn't find peace until every member of the Guiltless Gang had been brought to justice, and she couldn't do that while she was holed up in an Apache hut. But maybe she had a chance now – Cheveyo was leaving. She'd wait for a few minutes until she was sure he was gone, then she'd slip out. But as the seconds ticked by, Grace

91

found herself fighting to keep her eyes open. Had he tricked her with a sleeping potion? He'd only taken a small sip himself. No. She couldn't fall asleep… She had to stay awake… She had to get out of here…

Grace woke with a start. The room still smelled smoky, but daylight streamed through the doorway – the buffalo skin over the entrance was pulled aside. Twined burden baskets, pitch-covered vases, and clay pots lined the walls beside the door. Though still so weak she could barely push herself up on one elbow, Grace felt better. And she was alone.

Now was the time. She had to get out of here before Cheveyo returned.

But as soon as the thought crossed her mind, a shadow darkened the doorway. Grace's heart sank. If she'd only been a little faster…

"Glad to see you're finally awake."

"You again?"

"That's me. At least this time you aren't calling me *preacher*. My name is Joe, by the way. And you are?"

She pursed her lips, but then sighed and answered him. "Grace. Listen, is that Cheveyo gone? If he is we should get out of here now before he comes back—"

Joe interrupted her with a short, incredulous laugh.

"You can't go anywhere!"

"We have to!" The nervous energy running through Grace gave her voice a sharp edge. "What if … what if they scalp us?"

Joe threw back his head and laughed. "If they planned to do that, they'd have done it by now." He squatted down beside her. "Relax. You're in the medicine lodge. Lucky for you, Cheveyo's a skilled shaman. If it weren't for him, you would have died."

"We weren't captured? You brought me here *deliberately*? Why?"

"Don't you remember eating those pokeberries?"

She tried to nod but her head ached too much to move.

"For all his skills, Cheveyo was only just able to save you. Your fever got so high that you went wild. They had to lay you on the floor instead of on a bed." Joe gestured toward a rectangle of sticks woven into a mat and suspended from four stakes so it hung a foot off the floor.

It didn't look as if it would be any more comfortable than the ground.

"I … I wasn't sure you'd live." Joe glanced away and shook his head. "They even did the full healing ceremony with pollen and the Four Dancers."

"What?" Grace stared at him. "What did they do to me?"

"The Four Dancers danced around you for four days. Cheveyo sprinkled pollen on you."

Hazy memories of drums and pounding feet drifted back

93

to Grace. But then she realized something else Joe had said. "*Four* days? I've been out that long?"

"Longer than that. Your arm was infected. That and the pokeberries and not getting enough water. Lucky I found you when I did. You wouldn't have lasted much longer."

Grace bit back a retort. Who did he think he was? For some reason, he seemed to have appointed himself as her saviour. Although she did owe him her life and should feel grateful, his superior attitude annoyed her.

"Well, thank you for saving me again," she said through clenched teeth, but the words sounded far from gracious.

Joe grinned at her. "You're welcome. I'm glad I could help." He gave her a mock-stern look. "And I hope you learned your lesson and won't eat pokeberries again."

Would he ever let her live that down? "Anyone could have made that mistake."

"Not anyone with an ounce of sense. No one goes travelling in the desert without a knowledge of the dangers."

"My pa" – Grace's voice shook – "taught me about the dangers. It was one mistake."

"No slur on your pa, but he didn't teach you enough to survive alone out here. Knowing a few things about ranching life isn't enough to keep you alive in these hills. And it will never keep you alive tracking down outlaws like Hale."

What had she told him? How did he know what she intended to do? "What do you know of my plans?"

Grace demanded.

"Enough to know that you're plumb out of your skull. No one goes after criminals like Hale alone. And, even worse, unskilled." Joe shook his head. "Leave justice to the law."

"Why does everyone keep telling me to leave justice to others? First the preacher says to let God mete it out. Then Cheveyo says let … *Usen* do it. Now you, with the law!" Grace's chest heaved, and she clenched her good fist. "God didn't punish the Guiltless Gang. Why didn't he … I don't know, shoot lightning bolts from the sky? And how can I trust the *law*?" She spat the word. "Did any of them go after Hale? The sheriff ignored me." Grace's whole body shook with tremors of anger.

"I know," Joe said gently. "It's hard to watch criminals go unpunished."

"You have no idea."

"Actually, I do. And I know what it's like to feel the way you do. To be filled with grief and … and anger so strong it overwhelms you." Joe stared at the ground and shuffled his feet. "I couldn't help overhearing your screams and cries while you were feverish."

Grace's cheeks heated. She couldn't meet his eyes. What *had* she said?

"I know about what happened to your family. And why you want to get revenge. But Cheveyo's right. You must learn to let it go."

95

Grace's jaw clenched. She was about to burst out that he had no right to tell her what to do, but the deep sadness in Joe's eyes stopped her.

"I lost my family too," he said softly. "My mother died when I was seven, so Dad and Uncle Willis decided we ought to come out West to homestead." He had a tremor in his voice. "They never made it."

Grace frowned at him. "What do you mean?"

Joe sighed. "We were on a stagecoach heading toward Tombstone when bandits charged out of the hills. They held us up and shot the driver. Dad jumped out of the coach and confronted them while Uncle Willis lowered me out the window on the other side and told me to run toward a patch of trees and hide. He promised they'd follow. But … I heard the shots." A look of sickness crossed Joe's face, and he gazed off into the distance. "I stayed there in the scrub, scared and shivering, until the Indians found me."

Grace gasped. If he'd been a captive with the Indians all this time, there was little hope of escape.

"That wasn't the worst of it." Joe walked over to the wall and fingered a heavy ball of rawhide with a fringed buckskin handle that had a horsetail hanging from it. "See this?" he demanded.

Grace choked out a small "yes", hoping that the anger in his voice wasn't directed at her.

"The sheriff claimed they found a war club like this at the

scene." Joe punched a fist into his palm, and his voice was tight. "That was a lie. But the Indians got blamed. I couldn't identify their faces under those bandanas, because the only thing that showed were their eyes. Their cruel, mean eyes. But one thing I know for sure, they weren't Indians."

The pain in his voice brought tears to Grace's eyes.

"I didn't matter what I said though. The sheriff assembled a posse out to get the" – Joe choked out the word – "*Apache* who'd killed the stagecoach passengers." He turned his back and stood for a few moments, clenching and unclenching his jaw like he was trying to fight back tears. When his voice came again, it was thick. "They killed 27 Apache that day. Most of them women and children. Twenty-seven innocent people died, while the real killers went free. I got no so-called justice for my pa and uncle." He exhaled hard. "Yet in spite of that, the Ndeh took me in."

"Ndeh?"

Joe gestured toward the open doorway. "The Ndeh. You call them Apache, but they call themselves Ndeh. 'The people.'"

"You mean you *live* with the Apache? You're not a captive?"

He whirled on her, frowning. "Yes, I live with the Ndeh. They could have taken revenge for those deaths. Killed me to retaliate. Instead they adopted me. Treated me as if I were their own child. They taught me everything I know about survival, about life." He looked Grace straight in the eye. "And forgiveness."

Grace's brain was whirling. Everyone knew that the Apache were lawless savages. Everyone she knew always discussed them in hushed and fearful tones. Indians had attacked several ranches nearby; they were a constant threat. She just couldn't reconcile Joe's story with what she knew of their cruelty.

Joe held out a hand. "For years I wanted to track down my family's killers too. I was angry, like you."

"I'm not angry—"

But Joe continued as if he hadn't heard. "I kicked and fought those around me. Tried to keep them away. I'd vowed never to get close to anyone again."

Had Joe been eavesdropping on her conversation with the preacher?

"Since then I've watched others grieve. Raids have taken the lives of many in this band. And I do understand; anger helps you heal, it lets you know you're alive. But if you don't let it *go*, it poisons your soul."

"Now you really are sounding like the preacher," Grace scoffed.

"Then he's wise. Living with the Ndeh, I learned to let that anger go." Joe looked deep into Grace's eyes. "Stay for a while. Heal. Learn our ways. There is much they can teach you."

Joe's story and his pleading voice warmed a part of Grace's heart she'd thought was frozen. But she'd *never* be at peace if she accepted injustice. "I can't let those criminals go free. They might do the same thing to others. They have to be stopped.

And since no one else will, I intend to do it."

"What can one lone girl do against a gang of thieves and murderers?"

"I can find out where they're hiding and tell the deputy. I've heard at least *he's* honest." *Or I'll take care of it myself if he's not.*

"What if they find you first?"

"It's a chance I'll have to take."

Joe shook his head. "That's foolish." He paused, raising an eyebrow like he'd just thought of something. "If you stay here, the Ndeh can teach you how to stalk people so stealthily that they never know you're there. You can learn to use our weapons. Guns are fine at a distance, but if you're ambushed, you should know how to use a tomahawk, a knife, even a rock to defend yourself." Joe gave her a level stare. "Perhaps you might even discover you don't need revenge after all."

Grace let out an exasperated sigh. "I can't waste any more time. I may already be too late."

Joe motioned to the gun lying beside her. "You probably don't even know how to use that thing."

The gun? The Apaches hadn't stolen her gun? Grace's fingers closed gratefully around the cold metal on the ground beside her. She glared at Joe. "I bet I can shoot as well as you."

"Want to prove it? We could have a shooting contest."

Grace struggled to her knees, ignoring the whirling in her head. "I don't have time for contests. I need to get out of here."

"And I've told you, you aren't ready to go anywhere."

She'd show him. Grace pushed herself to her feet, but she would have pitched forward onto her face if Joe hadn't caught her. Still, she shook off his arm, setting off a shower of sparks in her brain. She stood for a few moments, willing the dizziness and nausea to subside. Then she took a few wobbly steps toward the opening. "Where's Bullet?"

"Your horse? He's being cared for. He was in worse shape than you. Cheveyo has done wonders, but that horse won't be ready to ride for weeks, maybe longer— Wait... Hey!"

Grace ignored him, lurching toward the doorway of the tent determinedly.

CHAPTER EIGHT

Joe caught up to Grace, his brow creased with concern. "Now, hold up a minute. I told you, both you and your horse need time to heal."

"I can't wait. I have to—" Grace stopped as she stepped out into the dazzling sunshine. She had to squint until her eyes adjusted to the brightness. When she opened them, all around her she saw women hard at work – tanning hides, slicing strips of meat from deer carcasses and draping them on drying racks over fires, pounding grain with stone mortars and pestles larger than the one the shaman had used. Many had cradleboards strapped to their backs, with babies peeking out from the semicircular buckskin hoods decorated with fringe and beadwork.

One of them could have been Zeke. Grace stood still and drew in a breath, trying to suck back the sob that threatened.

Children laughed and played. Some chased hoops with a sticks. Dogs barked and chased them. Others went racing past on horseback. They could have been Daniel and Abby. Women stirring pots over the fire reminded her of Ma hunched over the hearth… Grace's heart clenched into a tight knot. Families everywhere. And she was alone. Her loneliness merged with the ache that spread through her whole body.

It wasn't fair. Her whole family had been taken from her. She would never again gather vegetables for supper or pick berries for her family the way these girls were doing. She would never again sit down to a meal with her brothers and sister, or listen to Pa read at night, his deep voice soothing her to sleep. She would never again have anyone to touch, or hold, or care for her.

The Guiltless Gang had stolen everything from her. Everything of real value.

Grace could feel herself growing shakier as she stood watching the activity swirling around her – partly from her heartsickness, but her body *was* very weak. Still, determined not to prove Joe right, she shuffled one foot in front of the other, trying to rid herself of the quaking feeling.

Joe followed slowly at her side and cocked an eyebrow. "Not ready for this, are you?"

"I am so."

The corner of his mouth lifted. "Right, that's why you're dragging along. You can barely lift your feet. You're slower than a slug climbing the side of a water jar."

Grace gritted her teeth. She'd show him. She might not have the stamina to walk as fast as he could, but she'd be darned if she let him show her up in a shooting contest. And she wouldn't let him know she was still too ill to move any faster. "I'm … I'm just fascinated by the village, taking it all in. I've never seen Apaches close up." She hoped that sounded like a genuine excuse.

"Ndeh," Joe corrected. "Do you know what Apache means? It means 'enemy'. It's an insult. In fact, if you want to be more specific these are the Chiricahua people or the Chihuicahui. To the whites, all the so-called Apache are the same. But every band, every clan is different."

Grace didn't really feel like listening to a lecture from Joe, but at least it kept her mind off the pain of seeing Zeke in each papoose she passed. Or, wondering if Daniel would win among the young boys racing horses in the open field, their hair streaming behind them.

The women wore an odd mix of clothing. Some dressed in traditional buckskin poncho-like tops with a skirt tied at the waist, but others looked more like Mexican women, with tiered cotton skirts and puff-sleeved white blouses. Most had multiple strands of jewellery around their necks.

Grace wasn't the only one gawking. A few of the children had spotted her and they dropped their hoops or dismounted their horses, running over and crowding around her. They stared at her curiously, and some of the bolder ones reached up and touched her blonde braids with wonder in their eyes. Others poked at Grace's skin, giggling when they touched its paleness, and then looking down at their own brown skin. They chattered to each other excitedly, though some of the shyer children stayed in the background, gawping. Grace felt uncomfortable being the centre of attention, but she was grateful for the chance to stop and catch her breath.

Joe smiled. "They're fascinated by how blonde your hair is and how pale your skin is."

"I'm not pale," Grace protested. Ma had always despaired of Grace's skin, which had tanned to a golden brown from all the time she spent in the sun.

"Compared to me you are," Joe said with a grin, his teeth showing white in his swarthy face.

When Grace glanced at the mahogany-coloured hands stroking her arms, and the glossy black hair of everyone around her, she realized how strange she must appear to these children.

Joe barked something in a guttural tone and all but the boldest children backed away.

"What did you say?"

"I told them you were sick and needed to be left alone." He squatted down, said a string of strange words to the remaining

104

children, and pointed toward the women working near the wickiups. The children finally let go of Grace's arm and raced toward the women.

Joe chuckled. "I reminded them that their mothers needed help. I figured you wouldn't want an audience witnessing your humiliation in our shooting contest."

"You … you…" Grace sputtered, trying to find the words to put him in his place. She stalked ahead, ignoring her dizziness and wobbly legs. She'd show him – she was a good shot. Pa had taught her. She'd killed vermin and rattlesnakes; she'd be able to hit his stupid targets.

When they were far enough out of the village, Joe stopped. "We can shoot here without disturbing anyone."

"You go first." Grace was struggling to stay upright now. The walk had drained most of her strength. She needed a few minutes to stop the trembling in her legs and to clear her head, which felt wrapped in fog.

"You sure?" The corner of Joe's lips quirked again. "Shouldn't it be ladies first?"

Grace was so tired, she could hardly mumble. "I … I'll wait."

"If you're sure…" Joe waited for her nod, which set the pounding in her brain off harder than the warriors' drums. "I'll hit that first knothole. You can aim for the second one." He pointed to a distant branch and then lined up his shot.

Grace jumped at the sharp report and nearly fell. She

staggered back a few steps, trying to gain a firmer footing.

The target split in two. He'd hit dead centre.

If he could do it, so could she. She had to do this, prove to Joe she that wasn't a weakling, that she could take care of herself, that she was ready to get out of there.

Her arms were so weak and shaky she could barely lift the gun, let alone aim. She tried to focus her cloudy senses and took a deep breath, narrowing her eyes. But the target swayed, grew fuzzy around the edges. *Stay still*, she begged it. *Let me do this. Prove to Joe I can shoot.* She aimed at what she thought was the centre of the wavering knothole. Hoping she had it right, she squeezed the trigger. The impact travelled up her arm and knocked her backwards, and the report of the gun made Grace's teeth ache.

She would have tumbled to the ground if Joe hadn't caught her. His arms closed around her, keeping her upright. Grace wanted to shake him off, but dizziness closed in. Her grip on the gun loosened and it almost slid from her grasp. Her arms felt boneless, and she felt her body slide back against Joe's cradling arms. She willed herself to stand, finally breaking free and tottering away a few steps.

In the distance the target mocked her. She'd missed. She wasn't sure by how much, but… She shook off the hand Joe slid under her elbow to steady her again, gritting her teeth and willing the strange sensations to go away. The weakness, dizziness was making her mind whirl. After all her bragging, she'd humiliated herself. She hadn't even nicked the target.

Joe looked at her with concern, but could clearly see the determined clench in her jaw. "Uh, that shot went wild. Want to try again?" He looked like he was hoping she'd say no – like he was regretting even letting her try this challenge.

Grace's heart sank. She didn't want his pity, but she knew she wouldn't do any better with a second shot. Her head was reeling and her arm still shook from the first shot. The gun felt like it weighed so much she could hardly lift it, let alone steady it. Grudgingly, she shook her head, setting sparks shooting behind her eyes. But she still couldn't admit Joe was right. "I … I can't afford to waste the bullets. I may need them for protection." *Or to put through the hearts of murderers.*

"I can ride into town and get more bullets if you run out."

"No, no. I can't pay you and I already owe you too much already." She hadn't forgotten the pouch of silver he'd thrown to her.

"You don't owe me anything." Joe caught her gaze and held it. "Anyone with common decency would have done the same."

"But all that silver… I'll pay you back. I promise."

"Would you feel you owed me if I'd given you a load of firewood?"

Grace bit her lip. "No, probably not."

"So look around. The hills are filled with silver. Step into any stream and you'll find nuggets."

"You make it sound easy."

"It is. It's easier than finding kindling in the desert. Why do you think all the prospectors have flooded in, forcing the Ndeh from their homelands?" His tone turned savage. "Why do you think that gang tried to run your family off your ranch?"

And they'd succeeded. The land now lay empty, and no doubt prospectors would soon snap it up. All the time and effort and sweat Pa had invested. All gone. Grief rolled over Grace in waves. Pain. Anguish. The loss tore at her soul and she felt as if she were drowning, being sucked under the waves like she had been once as child when they'd lived back East. She had tumbled and tossed, not sure which way was up, while the waves had clawed at her chest, sucked her breath away. She felt like she being pulled under by huge waves now – only this time Pa wasn't there to rescue her.

"Grace?" Joe's tentative voice broke into her chaotic thoughts.

She shook herself free. "You … you were saying about the silver."

"Are you all right? Your skin looks really pale."

"Compared to *yours* maybe," she retorted with what she could muster of a grin. Joe faked a frown, but his eyes smiled back. She suddenly noticed that he'd stripped down to only his buckskin pants as the afternoon sun had grown stronger. Studying his brown, muscular shoulders gave Grace an odd queasy feeling in her stomach, and she glanced away and tried to compose herself. It was bad enough that she was light-

108

headed – she didn't need to add to it.

She had to change the subject. Taking a deep breath, she gritted her teeth and tried to stand straighter. "I'm fine. If I *did* have more bullets, I'd show you." She turned intending to stalk back to the teepee, but she swayed again.

Joe grabbed her elbow but she shook him off.

He shook his head at her stubbornness, but admiration gleamed in his eyes now. "Well, if you're *still* determined to prove yourself," he said, "we could use other weapons…"

She should turn him down. Walk – shuffle was more like it – back to the medicine lodge. But something inside of Grace refused to give up and admit defeat. "Like what?"

Joe studied her before he responded, as if gauging if she was serious. "Arrows or tomahawks."

Grace scoffed. "You'd have an unfair advantage!"

"So don't compare yourself to me. A straight shot is a straight shot, no matter what the weapon."

A bow and arrow would be lighter than the pistol that was weighing her arms down like a hundred-pound weight. "Fine."

Joe pressed his lips together. "All right then. I'll be right back."

Grace took a few grateful minutes to lean against a nearby tree and try and gather her strength, but soon Joe returned with a bow in one hand, a tomahawk in the other, and a quiver of arrows slung over his back. "You ever use a bow before?"

She shook her head, then instantly regretted it as the

109

pounding in her forehead intensified once more, and her vision blurred for a moment.

"Here, I'll show you," Joe said, removing an arrow from the beaded deerskin quiver on his back. He placed the feathered end of the arrow against the bowstring, then lined up the target and drew the string back slowly.

The arrow flew through the air and splintered the knothole he'd picked as Grace's target. He glanced at her. "You want me to show you again?" He pointed out a dangling pinecone, released another arrow, and it dropped to the ground.

That looked easy enough.

Joe handed her the bow and her arms shook slightly as she took it from him. Grace assured herself that it was only from weakness. She tried to imitate the proper position he'd shown her, but as she did so Joe reached out and closed a hand over hers.

"Move this one closer to the centre." He nudged her hand up, then glanced down at her – he was so close the sunlight seemed to turn his dark eyes to amber. "You'll have to stay steadier than that if you want to hit a target."

Grace clenched her jaw and willed the shakiness to subside as Joe's hand drew hers and the bowstring back.

"Now aim," Joe commanded. "Steady … fire!"

He'd startled her so much that she let go of the bowstring too early and the bow tilted, sending the arrow shooting straight up to the air. It lodged in a tree branch overhead, where it hung quivering mockingly. Grace sucked in a deep breath of irritation that started her coughing and sputtering.

Joe patted her back. "You OK?"

"Fine, fine," Grace choked out. She waved a hand to move him away. How would she learn to shoot with his body pressed against hers? When he returned with the arrow, Grace practically snatched it from him.

"I want to try it myself. I'll never learn if someone else does it for me."

Joe held up his hands in surrender but gave her a few instructions as Grace reloaded the arrow. She adjusted her position until he was satisfied.

"Now, just pull back the bowstring, aim at the target, and let it fly."

But Grace's weakened muscles could barely drag the bowstring back a few inches. The string twanged away from her and the arrow nosedived into the ground in front of her. She sighed, expecting Joe to make a quip, but he just rushed over and picked the arrow up. Grace smiled gratefully. She hadn't been sure she could manage it on her shaky legs.

"Sure you don't want me to help you for a while?" Joe said quietly.

"I can do it." Grace bit out each word. Her response sounded ungracious so she added, "I appreciate your help, but..." Joe shrugged and she loaded the arrow again. But after several mishaps – arrows embedded into the ground by

111

her feet and two shots that went wide – Grace finally had to admit defeat. What made her heart sink to the floor was that Joe was right. She really wasn't well enough or strong enough yet to track Hale's gang. If she'd taken off as she'd planned, she'd probably have slipped from Bullet's back and collapsed in a heap within an hour. Her mind went back to the wolves circling. The vultures overhead. She shivered.

"Cold?" Joe asked.

Grace jerked back to the present – she'd been far away, collapsed by a stream as coyotes nosed her still body. Tiredness suddenly overwhelmed her. "I … I think I should lie down."

Joe reached out to steady her again. "Plumb tuckered out, ain't you? Told you—" He broke off abruptly. Grace's legs were quivering like a sapling buffeted by desert winds, and as she took a step forward, she stumbled – but before she fell, Joe scooped her into his arms. His eyes softened as he looked down at her. "I was foolish to challenge you like this. Just me being stupid, trying to prove a point." He shook his head. "Let's get you back to the medicine lodge."

"Put me down!" Grace had intended to snap out the order, but instead it came out soft and hesitant. "Now," she commanded, but Joe ignored her and strode on toward the centre of camp. "I can walk," Grace protested weakly.

Joe's jaw tightened. "Yeah? You're shivering like a deer with an arrow lodged in its side."

"I am not—"

"If you get sicker, it'll be all my fault. I should never have taunted you that way."

"I wanted to do it…" Grace mumbled, struggling to form words with uncooperative lips.

"Hush. Save your breath. You can argue with me when you're well. I want a worthy opponent. Not one who's staggering like she's downed too much firewater."

Firewater! Grace meant to say the word, but her lips wouldn't form the words. She felt as if she'd been *dipped* in firewater.

As they reached the medicine tent and Joe laid her down on the mat, Cheveyo glared at him. "What have you done to her?"

"She did it to herself with her foolish claims that she was ready to leave." The soft soothing voice he'd used as he'd carried her toward the medicine lodge now held a note of defensiveness.

"Ah." Cheveyo's one word carried both forgiveness and warning. "She is still much too weak to be up."

Joe hung his head. "I know. It is my fault for taunting her. Will she be all right?"

"Many nights of healing can be undone by such foolishness." Cheveyo sighed. "Though her mind is strong and determined as an oak, her body cannot yet support those thoughts. If only I could pull the poison of revenge from her mind, she would quiet and heal more quickly. But she is like an unbroken colt, pulling and chafing at the ropes that bind it."

Cheveyo's words floated around Grace as if they came from a great distance, muffled by the thick fog engulfing her.

And soon they swirled off into nothingness.

CHAPTER NINE

The next day, after Cheveyo left, Joe ducked through the doorway.

Grace looked up drowsily and saw that he stood head bowed, hands clasped in front of him.

"I came to apologize."

"For what?" Grace's words came out thickly past the lump in her throat. She couldn't look at him, remembering yesterday. She'd made a fool of herself.

Joe shuffled his moccasins in the dirt. "I knew you weren't well, but I goaded you into that competition. And now I've made you even sicker."

"It's not your fault," she mumbled. Now that she'd

recovered some of her strength, she couldn't believe she'd let him carry her that way – she knew her ma would have told her that's no way for a lady to behave. But he showed none of the awkwardness and embarrassment that she struggled with inside. The evenness of his voice, the clearness of his tone revealed that last night had been nothing more than a chore for him. He'd taken care of her the same way he'd take care of a little girl if she'd fallen and scraped her knee.

"Well, I should have known better. And I'm very sorry." He turned to leave.

"Joe?"

He turned, his face both expectant and wary.

"I… Never mind." She infused a flatness into the words. "It really wasn't your fault. I wanted to prove myself." Which she hadn't done – so as much as she hated to admit it, she forced herself to add, "And you were right."

Joe gave a wry smile. "Yeah, well, I wish I wasn't." He ducked through the opening, leaving her alone. *What did he mean by that? He wants me to go?* Grace rolled her eyes at herself. What she needed to focus on was getting better so she could get out of there.

A few hours later, Joe popped back into the medicine lodge holding a pelt. "Oh. Where's Cheveyo? He wanted this."

Grace wrinkled her nose. "What is that awful smell?"

Joe's cheeks turned ruddy. "I've just come from hunting." He motioned to the grease slathered all over his chest, face, and hair. "We cover ourselves with animal fat to mask our human scent. That way the prey can't smell us stalking them."

"Makes sense, I guess," Grace said, holding her nose. "But I hope you plan to take a bath soon."

"Right after I take you to meet someone." Joe left the pelt in a corner of the lodge and came over to help Grace to her feet. Cheveyo's warning not to overdo things was running through her mind, but she stood up a bit steadier on her feet this time and accompanied Joe into the village.

He led her over to one of the girls about her age. "This is Sequoyah. Her name means 'Sparrow'." He gestured toward Grace. "Sequoyah, this is our visitor, Grace." He smiled at the girl, who ducked her head shyly.

"I am … pleased to meet you," Sequoyah said, then she looked to Joe as if for approval.

He nodded. "You said it right."

A relieved smile crossed her face. "The English I am learning. Sometimes I do not say it the right way, but Joe, he help me."

Grace couldn't help smiling back at the girl's infectious grin. "I'm pleased to meet you too."

"I hope you will help me with the English too." She threw a teasing glance at Joe. "He often too busy to help."

"He *is* often too busy," Joe corrected.

"*Is*. I remember. It is hard. Much hard."

"*Very* hard." Joe said.

Sequoyah smiled ruefully. "I need much practice. English very hard." She clapped a hand to her mouth. "*English is very hard*. See, Joe, I do it right."

He grinned. "You're doing a fine job." Joe turned to Grace. "If you need anything, just ask. Sequoyah knows everything around here."

Sequoyah dipped her head and looked at the ground. "I not…" Her words stumbled to a halt, then she started again. "I *do* not know everything. Joe, he is making joke."

"You know a lot," Joe said. "I know Grace will be in good hands."

Sequoyah looked up, a puzzled frown creasing her brow. She held out her palms. "She cannot fit in my hands."

Joe burst out laughing, and Grace hid a smile. "It's just an English expression. It means you will take good care of Grace."

Sequoyah's tan cheeks grew rosy. "Oh. I understand." She turned to Grace. "That is expression Joe taught me. Now that you are here, I will have two people to help me. I will learn much better."

"I'd love to help you, but I won't be here for too long."

"But Joe say…?"

Grace glared at Joe. He had no business telling people what her plans were when he didn't even know himself. "I have business to attend to. I will be on my way soon." As soon as she could put one wobbly foot in front of the other. As soon as she could stand without starting to feel dizzy. And as soon as she could shoot straight again. But *soon*.

After Joe left for his bath in the stream, Sequoyah put a gentle hand on Grace's arm. "Joe tell me about your family. I am very much sorry. It is hard to lose the people you love." Her faraway expression spoke of great sadness. "The soldiers killed my mother and my baby brothers. I was…" She held out a hand about three feet from the ground.

"Small?" Grace asked.

Sequoyah nodded. "Yes, I was much – *very* – small. Many of my people die that day." Her voice wavered, but then she brightened a little. "Soon after that Joe came. My father, he adopted Joe. Joe's family dead too."

"I know. Joe told me." Grace's heart went out to Sequoyah too. They had all lost those closest to them. And all because of some men who were allowed to murder and get away with it. The posse who'd slaughtered Joe's family, then Sequoyah's. Was it the same men? Grace had no idea, but she couldn't stand all these evil men being allowed to kill and get away without punishment. She wouldn't let that happen to her family's killers. "That is why I cannot stay, Sequoyah. I must find the men who murdered my family. Bring them to justice."

"But you are still ill. And … you are a girl."

Perhaps Sequoyah was right. "But there's no one else

to do it," Grace said.

"In our band, we might fight if attacked, but women do not go off on their own. Bad things happen. The people around here are cruel. Not just the soldiers, but the white men. And the Mexicans. They do things to our women…" She looked away, her jaw set. "I do not know the words for this. But it is bad. Very bad. They act like we are animals."

Grace knew the word Sequoyah was searching for, but it was not a word she wanted to teach her new friend. The ugliness of what she'd described made Grace even more certain that those outlaws must be stopped. If no one else was brave enough, it would *have* to be her.

Sequoyah ran a hand along Grace's tattered sleeve. The bear had shredded it, and Grace had torn most of her skirt into strips for bandages and a net. Her father's cut-down buckskin leggings were covered with stains that she hadn't been able to scrub out at the bordello, and her bodice was stained with sweat from the fever. She'd told Joe he stunk but she realized now that she probably smelled worse.

"You need some clothes." Sequoyah held out her arm to Grace. "Come. I get you some."

She walked slowly to keep pace with Grace's hesitant, careful steps and then ducked into a dome-shaped brush-covered building similar to the medicine lodge, leading Grace in with her.

"My home, *kuugh'a*," she said.

Grace tried the word.

Sequoyah giggled and repeated it a few times until Grace said it well. "Joe, he call our *kuugh'a* a wickiup. That is funny word."

Grace glanced around at the strips of meat dangling from the rafters, the tan baskets with black diamond shapes woven into them, the pitch-covered vases, the fur and deerskins tossed on the matting beds.

Sequoyah touched her arm, startling Grace from her inspection. "I give you a skirt and…" She gestured toward her chest and arms.

"Blouse?"

"Yes." She patted Grace's arm and shoulder. "Your blouse is ripped. You need new one."

"But I can't take your clothes."

"These are old. I have new ones." Sequoyah twirled so her three-tiered cotton skirt swirled out around her. "The men trade with the Mexicans for clothes. But I keep the others. Some things easier to do in these."

She held out a poncho-like shirt of soft deerskin with beaded designs and a deer tail hanging in back. She showed Grace how to wrap the large piece of soft buckskin around her waist for a skirt.

"But I'm too dirty to wear these."

"A wash? You need a wash."

Grace nodded.

Sequoyah looked at her. "This mean yes?" She bobbed her head up and down. "And this mean no." She moved her head from side to side in slow motion.

"That's right," Grace said with a smile. She had never realized how hard it could be to communicate when two people spoke different languages. Even things as simple as gestures for *yes* or *no* were not the same. She wasn't sure if Sequoyah understood enough to answer her questions, but she'd ask Joe to teach her some of the Apache gestures. *Ndeh*, she corrected herself.

"Come. I take you to the water." She picked up a small clay jar. "Yucca. Good for—" Sequoyah rubbed her hands together and pantomimed scrubbing her hair and body.

"Soap?" Grace asked.

"Yes, yes. Soap."

When they reached the bank of the stream, Joe had just pulled on his buckskin leggings. His tanned, wet back glistened, and Grace couldn't help staring. When he turned, she swallowed hard, embarrassed. Until she'd come here, she'd never seen a man without a shirt on. But the warriors in the camp hadn't made her stomach somersault. The braves had no chest hair, but the damp whorls of hair on Joe's chest fascinated her.

Sequoyah nudged her. "Take your wash."

"I-I can't. Not until Joe's gone."

Sequoyah looked startled. "Why?"

"I'm not taking my clothes off in front of him,"

Grace whispered.

"I do not understand."

She stared at Sequoyah. "You'd undress in front of men? Let them see you naked – without clothes?"

"But that is how Usen made you." Sequoyah laughed. "Babies not born with clothes on."

Grace wasn't sure about that. Abby and Zeke had never gone without clothes unless they were getting their diapers changed. But she had noticed that many of the Ndeh children ran around naked.

Sequoyah called over to Joe. "You must go. Ger-race not take bath with you here."

Joe's cheeks reddened, but they were no match for the heat enveloping Grace's face by now.

"Oh … of course not," Joe said. His Adam's apple bobbed up and down as if he were swallowing hard. "The English do things differently than the Ndeh." His words came out a bit husky.

Hastily, he slid his moccasins over his feet and up his legs, cuffing them at the top and sliding a knife into one side. Then he reached down and swiped up his buckskin shirt, his parfleche, and his beaded necklaces quickly. He squashed them under one arm, and with the other he picked up his hat and set it on his still-damp hair. "Uh, good day, ladies." He hurried up the bank as if he couldn't get away fast enough.

"*Now* you can wash." Sequoyah grinned and handed

Grace the yucca.

Was she going to stand here and watch? Grace had never bathed in front of anyone but her mother during their weekly Saturday night baths. She turned her back and started to slip off her leggings, but when she bent, the ground whirled before her eyes. She pitched forward, and from a distance she heard Sequoyah call out, but Grace couldn't make out the words.

Gentle hands lowered her to the ground. "You should be in bed." Sequoyah's scolding words in English were followed by a string in a language of strange sounds with varying pitches and tones.

"I … I'm all right." Grace pushed herself upright with her good arm. "Just a little dizzy, that's all."

"I call Joe to help?"

"No, no, don't do that. I can do this myself." Grace forced herself to stand, and then walked slowly toward the stream. She decided she'd take her clothes off once she was in there.

The shock of the icy water made Grace gasp, but it cleared her head a bit. She grabbed an overhanging branch to keep herself steady and realized that her palms didn't sting any more. She studied her sore arm. The skin was mostly pink with a few blotches of dead, peeling skin. But her injuries had been coated with an ointment of some kind. Cheveyo must be a magician. Or would her hands have healed the same on their own, given time? Joe had never answered her question about how long she'd been at the camp.

She struggled to free herself from the sopping-wet clothes dragging her down, and when she threw them on the bank, Sequoyah handed her the yucca.

Grace scrubbed away layers of grime and sweat with relief. The cool, clear water and mild scent of the suds brought back memories of the hipbath at the bordello – and then of her family's Saturday night baths. Zeke went first, then Abby. Pa and Daniel always left the house, and after Grace had her bath she waited for Ma on the porch. Pa's pipe glowed against the evening sky while he and Daniel waited near the barn. When Ma emerged, Pa and Daniel took their turns—

"Ger-race?" Sequoyah's voice brought her back to the present.

No Ma. No Pa. No… Grace turned away and splashed water on her face to stop the tears that threatened to fall.

"Yes, I'm coming," Grace choked out. She pulled herself out of the water and staggered up the bank.

With Sequoyah's help, she donned the dry clothes, and Sequoyah rolled and tied up one blouse sleeve so the buckskin wouldn't rub against Grace's infected arm. With her old, sopping-wet clothes in one hand, Sequoyah used her other to help Grace up the bank. "Now we will help you build a *kuugh'a*."

Grace explained that it might not be worth the trouble as she wouldn't be there long but Sequoyah brushed aside her protests. "You cannot go soon. Your horse must heal.

And so must you."

Too tired to argue, Grace followed Sequoyah to the spot the women had chosen for her home. Bathing and walking back from the stream had sapped Grace's energy, and she sank to the ground as soon as they arrived.

Several women rushed over and began cutting saplings. They tied them together quickly to form the dome shape of the *kuugh'a*.

"Ask them to wait until I can help," Grace said to Sequoyah.

But Sequoyah only shook her head. "You are ill. This time you watch. Next time you help."

Within a short while, a matting of dried grasses covered the frame. One of the women dug a hole in the centre of the floor, while others spread that dirt around the lower edges of the *kuugh'a*.

At Grace's questioning glance, Sequoyah explained. "The hole is for your fire. The dirt, it keep—" She held her hands in the air and wriggled her finger downward.

"Rain?" Grace asked.

"Yes, rain." Sequoyah smiled. "It keep rain out. You stay nice and dry."

Grace memorized every step of the construction. She wouldn't be here long, but she was determined to help if anyone else needed to build another *kuugh'a* while she was there. And she had another reason for paying such close attention – she wouldn't have buffalo skin to throw over the top of the shelter the way the women had done here, but she'd do well to know how to build herself a shelter while she was tracking down the Guiltless Gang.

She was lost in her thoughts, barely hearing Sequoyah's explanation of why doorways faced east and how the Ndeh tied their belongings to the dogs, moving camp often so they could stay near the best sources of food.

One woman gathered wood, piled it in the hole in the centre of the *kuugh'a*, and lit the fire. Others stacked more wood and dried brush near the opening, which they hung with deerskin as a makeshift doorway.

Within a short while, the *kuugh'a* was complete. Grace asked Sequoyah to thank everyone for her. Sequoyah broke into another series of sounds and tones that sounded strange, but musical, to Grace's ears, and the women smiled shyly at her, said a few words to Sequoyah, and then returned to their own homes.

Sequoyah turned to Grace. "They said they hope you are much happy here and that you will stay with us. You are now a part of our family."

Grace looked away, choking up. Sequoyah's words touched the lonely part of her deep inside. But Grace had her *own* family to think about. And she had a mission to stick to.

CHAPTER TEN

When Joe came to get Grace a little while later, his eyebrows rose at the sight of her buckskin top and skirt. "You look … different."

Grace chuckled at his expression. "I look clean."

"Uh, Sequoyah sent me to get you," Joe said. "Everyone is ready to eat. Come and join us."

She shook her head. "I've taken too much from the Ndeh already."

"Grace, you need to eat, to keep up your strength."

"I do not want everyone staring at me."

"It's just because you're a novelty with your blonde hair." The way his eyes travelled over its now-shining ripples gave

Grace the impression it attracted him as well. "And your skin is so soft and white."

Now she was even more embarrassed. She shook her head again, but Joe was having none of it.

"Listen, it's rude to decline an invitation to eat. You will offend those who have been kind to you."

She couldn't do that. Reluctantly, she followed Joe from her new *kuugh'a* to where everyone was assembled. The scent of roasting meat wafted from the fire and Grace inhaled deeply. After so many days of being ill, her stomach longed for a taste, and the flatbread many of the children were nibbling looked delicious.

"Come." Joe led her over to Sequoyah's side.

The girl smiled and gestured for Grace to help herself. In addition to the meat and bread, painted gourd and pottery bowls were heaped with chokecherries and wild plums. Everything looked delicious.

The younger children stopped eating and stared at Grace. Self-conscious, she smoothed down her hair and waited until they all got absorbed in eating again before she tasted the foods on the table. She wasn't well or strong enough to eat much, but she appreciated every bite.

As she ate, she leaned closer to Sequoyah. "Thank you so much for the clothes."

"You look pretty," Sequoyah said. "Joe like them, I think."

"I don't know…"

Sequoyah's teasing grin indicated that she didn't believe her.

A few minutes later, Joe came over and sat beside Grace, helping to translate the conversation around the table. Every time he leaned close to talk to her, a young man with a badly scarred chest scowled at him.

Grace elbowed Joe. "That brave over there seems angry with you."

"Umm-hmm." Joe kept his voice low. "That's Tarak. Cheis adopted him soon after he adopted me, so we're blood brothers. I think he's upset because I said that I plan to train you to be a warrior."

A warrior? Was that how Joe saw her? Grace smiled and sat up straighter, trying to look more warrior-like. "I'm sorry I've caused trouble between you and your brother. But I do want to learn the Ndeh ways, and if you're really willing to teach me that would be much appreciated."

"Well, that's not the only thing that's upsetting him." He frowned, tore off a chunk of the flat round bread he called *chigustei*, and dipped it into his soup.

But before Grace could get up the courage to ask him what he meant, the meal ended.

After they'd finished eating, the men gathered in a circle with a long pipe Joe called a *calumet*. A peace pipe. Feathers dangled from it along with tufts of horsehair and animal fur.

Joe gestured toward the man holding the pipe. "That's Cheis, Sequoyah's father."

Grace stared at the imposing figure, who sat so still he could have been carved from wood. "Is he the chief?"

"The Ndeh don't really have chiefs. They believe each man should decide for himself what is right. The men meet and make decisions together, and when they do, they often look to the wisest man for counsel. In this band, that's Cheis." Joe stood. "If you plan to be a warrior, why don't you join us in smoking the pipe?"

None of the other women had joined the group so Grace shook her head, but once Joe joined the men, he patted the ground beside him and beckoned to her. She was about to refuse when she caught sight of Tarak glaring at her. She'd show him. If she planned to be a warrior, she would act like a warrior, whether that angry brave liked it or not. Pushing herself unsteadily to her feet, she walked over and sat beside Joe. She couldn't sit cross-legged in her skirt, so she tucked her legs under her.

Cheis closed his eyes and murmured prayers while Joe whispered the words to Grace. After sprinkling a bit of tobacco to the east, Cheis repeated it in each of the other three directions.

"The Four Directions are sacred," Joe whispered. "Next, he will offer tobacco to Mother Earth and Father Sky."

Cheis patted the ground and set some tobacco by his feet, then lifted his hands skyward and tossed a bit of tobacco overhead. When the prayers ended, Cheis held his hand open until the last bits of tobacco floated away on the wind.

Then he sat in the circle with the others. One eyebrow raised in surprise when he caught sight of Grace, but he quickly composed his features. "Ah. We welcome newcomer to our tribe."

Tarak's eyes blazed with anger. His fury could have lit the pipe, but his adopted father did the honours. Cheis passed the pipe to the man next to him and Grace watched carefully to see what the others did. They sucked lightly at the pipe, then blew out a bit of smoke. She relaxed a little. It looked easy enough.

The pipe reached Joe, who did what the others had done.

When Joe handed it to Grace, Cheis spoke again in halting English: "It make no difference as to the name of your God ... because love is real God of all the world. Even your silence ... holds a prayer."

Grace smiled her thanks, unsure what to say in response. Although she had all but denounced God, she appreciated Cheis's words and the fact that he was accepting her.

"He is extending the tribe's peace and protection to you," Joe whispered.

Grace took the long carved stick with the stone bowl. Smoke rose from the end, and she sucked on the pipe in the way she'd seen the others do. Smoke filled her lungs, burned her nostrils and mouth, and she choked, coughing and spluttering and trying to draw in a breath. Tears stung her eyes, and Joe

132

patted her back.

"You all right? You aren't supposed to inhale the smoke into your lungs, just hold it in your mouth," he whispered.

The man next to her took the pipe from her hand, but did not smoke it. Instead he joined Joe in making sure she was OK.

Everyone sat solemnly, waiting until she recovered. All except one person. Tarak clutched his belly and laughed silently. Even after the pipe began making its rounds again, Tarak continued to gaze at Grace and snicker, but Cheis gave him a stern look and he sobered. But when Cheis's attention focused elsewhere, Tarak smirked at Grace once more.

As soon as the ceremony ended and the musicians gathered for dancing, Grace could finally get away without seeming rude. She fled to her *kuugh'a*, cringing that she'd made a fool of herself again, and likely shamed Joe in the process. She wished she could mount Bullet and gallop from the camp. Never have to face anyone again. *Oh, Bullet, hurry and get well.*

The drum pounded out a beat, and soon feet slapping on the earth accompanied the musicians. No one would miss her now. Grace lay on her reed bed and stared up at the smokehole, watching the sky turn grey and night fall.

In the doorway someone cleared his throat, and Grace jumped.

"May I come in?"

Joe. Grace's heart raced faster than the drumbeats that

133

shook the earth under her feet. "Wh-what are you doing here?"

"I came to get you. You don't want to miss your first dance."

Oh, yes, I do. Grace was sure of that. She'd had enough humiliation for one night. And she didn't need to see Tarak's smirks. "I'm tired. I need to sleep."

"But you'll enjoy it. The storytelling is fascinating – I promise to translate. Why don't we just sit somewhere on the edge of the crowd?" He suppressed a smile. "They've put the *calumet* away…"

Grace crossed her arms. "Did you do that on purpose to embarrass me?"

Joe's face fell. "I wouldn't do that! But you have to admit, you did look pretty funny…"

The twinkle in his eye made Grace smile. "I guess so." But she couldn't help adding ruefully, "I bet no one's ever done that before."

"Someone must have in all the years they've been doing the *calumet* ceremony. If not, you may become part of their stories." He grinned and reached for her hand. "Come listen to them."

When his fingers touched hers, a tingle ran up her arm. Grace pulled her hand away a little too quickly, and a frown creased Joe's brow. "Oh. I'm so sorry. I forgot about your palms." He reached out and cupped her upturned hand gently in his strong, calloused one, inspecting. "They look much better though. That salve Cheveyo put on worked well. When

134

I brought you here, they were blistered and raw." His voice held a note of tenderness. "You were very brave to fight through the fire like that."

The look of admiration he gave her set her cheeks aflame, and she lowered her eyes, confused. The tenderness of Joe's touch had her so mixed up, she wanted to cry and smile at the same time.

"I wish – I wish I'd stayed around when my pa…" His voice broke. "I never even knew where they were buried…" He shook his head as if to dislodge the memories. "Let's go and dance."

Grace's breath had gotten stuck somewhere inside her chest, making her lungs ache. Her words came out whispery. "I don't know how."

"It's easy." He slipped an arm around her shoulders and led her to the doorway. "Look. The women shuffle one way. The men the other." He moved into the shadow of some overhanging trees. "We can try it here where no one can see you."

After a few false starts, Grace picked up the rhythm of the drum and the slapping of bare feet. *Stomp, stomp, stomp. Jingle.* Repeat. She almost laughed.

He smiled back. "Want to join them?"

Grace glanced at the dancers and spotted Sequoyah eyeing one of the musicians.

"We could slip in beside her," Joe said, following

Grace's gaze.

"All right." Grace let him lead her toward the crowd.

Just before they reached the dancers, Cheis stepped out of line. He walked over and laid a hand on Sequoyah's head, then leaned down to whisper something in his daughter's ear, his smile tender – the way Pa used to look at her. The way he'd never look at her again.

An ache built in her chest. She couldn't bear to watch, but couldn't tear her gaze away. Her eyes stung, misting the images of father and daughter. She couldn't cry, not here, not now. Not in front of everyone.

Grace yanked her hand from Joe's. She turned and ran, her lungs burning, her chest aching, her weakened muscles protesting hard. She stumbled, and her legs almost gave out, but she kept going until she reached the pasture.

Far below, the town of Tombstone appeared in miniature. Too small to even see people walking the streets as dusk closed in. Off to the south lay scarred land and her family's homestead, now only a blackened smudge on the red clay.

And behind it lay a mound.

From here all Grace could make out was a small brown blob that might have been the cross she'd made, or maybe it was only a speck of dust in her eye. She blinked to clear her vision, but the scene only grew more blurry. Her eyes filmed over with moisture until the whole landscape became indistinct.

A whinny from across the pasture caught her attention.

"Bullet!"

The horse hobbled toward her, and Grace flung her arms around his neck and buried her face in his mane, careful not to bump against his torn side or bandaged legs.

"Oh, Bullet, it hurts so much. I can't bear it."

Bullet's quiet whicker sounded sympathetic.

"You miss them too, don't you?" Grace breathed in the warmth and comfort of horseflesh. The ache in her chest expanded until it turned into gasps, and the tears she'd dammed back threatened to overflow.

She had no idea how long she stood there, gulping back sobs, before a gentle hand touched her shoulder. When she turned and saw the understanding look in Joe's eyes, all the tears she been holding back streamed down her face. She cried until her tears were spent, then sank to the ground, exhausted and dry-eyed, staring into the distance.

The sky darkened and the stars came out.

Still Joe sat beside her, silently.

CHAPTER ELEVEN

A loud argument startled Grace awake at dawn. Though she couldn't understand the words, the tone was unmistakable. She peeked her head out of her *kuugh'a* anxiously – after the merriment of the previous evening and the kindness of the tribe, it shocked her to hear such hostility.

Sequoyah spotted her looking out and hurried over. "I am sorry they woke you."

Grace rubbed her puffy, sore eyes and tried to make sense of the crowd of angry men. They all seemed to be directing their ire toward one scowling man who stood, legs planted defiantly, apart from the group. "What's happening?"

"That is Tall Tree. He not take care of parents as he should.

He is bad. Very bad. Good sons help parents. Feed them, fix the *kuugh'a*…"

"But what are they doing to him?" Grace asked as one of the men pointed to the woods and gave Tall Tree a shove.

"Joe say white men put bad men behind bars. Like in cages. That is called prison?" Sequoyah looked at Grace with a question in her eyes as if asking for confirmation.

Grace nodded. She supposed prisons were like cages. Cages she'd like to see filled with the faces of her family's murderers. "So you do not have prisons?"

"No. We send the bad ones out into the wilderness. It is sad, but Tall Tree did not listen to the council. They give him many chances."

After Tall Tree vanished into the woods, life at the camp resumed as normal. But Grace couldn't get him out of her mind, especially after Sequoyah explained that those who were banished could never join another band. He was destined to live life alone. The way she was – though she'd done nothing wrong.

Her sense of loneliness only increased as the women began preparing breakfast for their children. Families gathered to eat, and Grace ducked into her *kuugh'a* before any of them saw her and motioned for her to join them. Her heart hurt too much to sit with a happy family group.

But a short while later, another commotion began. This time, though, the noise was only a small group of men gathering to go hunting. Looking out, she saw that Joe was among them, and she hurried over to him.

"Could I come along with you? It would be good training for me. I could watch and see how you track game, or—"

Just then, one of the hunters rushed over to Joe and grabbed his arm. Grace recognized his face – and his badly scarred chest. Tarak. He chattered rapidly to Joe, sending angry glances toward her. When he gestured toward their weapons and then jabbed a finger in Grace's direction, she tugged on Joe's arm, frowning. "What's he saying?" She knew whatever it was wouldn't exactly be complimentary.

Joe sighed. "He doesn't want me to teach a white girl Ndeh ways."

Tarak glared at her with narrowed eyes as Joe spoke.

"Well, tell him— Wait! Does he understand English?"

"A bit. He understood that you were asking to come along on the hunt."

"Then I'll tell him myself." Grace turned and met the fury of Tarak's gaze with her own icy glare. "If someone killed your family, you would take revenge. I am the only one left to get justice. So I must learn."

Tarak growled something that Joe did not bother to translate.

Grace folded her arms and persevered. "Sequoyah told me about Gouyen, the woman who killed the Comanche chief to avenge her husband's death. Joe said it's a true story. If she can

140

get revenge, so can I."

Tarak refused to answer her in English, but what he did say, he practically spat. Grace took a step back at his angry tone.

"What did he say?" she asked Joe, not taking her eyes off Tarak.

"You don't want to know. But he is upset that you compared yourself to a Ndeh heroine when you are not Ndeh."

"So I'll compare myself to … to…" Grace couldn't think of any white women who had avenged their families. In their cabin, though, *Foxe's Book of Martyrs* stood on the fireplace mantel with the Bible and the primer. She narrowed her eyes. "Tell him I'm like Joan of Arc."

But before Joe had gotten out more than a few words, Tarak stalked off – not before sending one more hate-filled glance her way.

Grace shivered. She clearly had at least one enemy in this camp. How many more were less open about it? She shook her head, irritated. What had she done to anger him? She turned to Joe. "Why does he hate me so much?"

"It's not you. It's any paleface. He lost his whole family in that raid I told you about. The soldiers tortured and killed his father, then…" He hesitated, looking at Grace. "Then they raped his mother and sister before slitting their throats. The whole time two men held Tarak down, forcing him to watch. Afterwards they tortured and knifed Tarak and left him for dead. He still bears the scars."

141

Grace stared at Tarak's retreating back. So that was the reason for the ugly scars on his chest. The scars inside must be worse.

Joe continued, "Cheis adopted him the same way he adopted me."

At least he *had* a family to take him in. That was more than Grace had. "So he hates me because I'm a paleface? We're not all the same, you know."

Joe raised an eyebrow at her. "Well, remember how you thought of the Apache?"

Grace sighed. "I guess you're right."

He stared off into the distance. "From the first, he hated me for the colour of my skin. And when Cheis adopted me, he made my life miserable until Cheis found out and made him stop. I think now he's worried that Cheis will adopt you."

"I hope you made it clear that I don't intend to stay. As soon as Bullet is well enough to travel, I'll be on my way."

"I haven't had a chance. You saw how he walked away." Joe smacked his fist into his palm. "He does that any time I try to talk to him."

While Grace and Joe talked, the hunters farther down the path talked among themselves, and then one approached Joe. The two of them talked seriously for a few minutes and then Joe nodded. He turned to Grace. "They have asked me to tell you to stay with the women. Gather wood, pick nuts and berries, scrape buffalo hides."

"And you agreed with them?" Grace's words were edged with indignation.

"I've already explained how the Ndeh decide things, Grace," he said, though she could tell he felt conflicted. "It's a group decision. The hunters don't want a girl to join them. I'm sorry."

Grace pinched her lips together to hold back an angry retort. It wasn't Joe's fault, but it still made her blood boil.

Joe held out an imploring hand. "Try to understand. Ndeh women can hunt small game – woodrats or rabbits – but they don't go on hunts like this. We're not just doing a short hunt; we'll be gone for days. And we'll be sneaking through enemy territory." His eyes glittered. "This is the first bison hunt the band has attempted for a long time. You can't blame them for not wanting a new hunter along."

"But—" The word burst out of her, but before she could finish, Joe held up a hand.

"I know, I know. You're a good hunter. Not as good as me, of course." He grinned to show he was joking.

One of the men beckoned impatiently. Joe gave her a brief wave and then hurried to catch up with the other men, who were making their way out of the camp.

Grace ground her teeth. She'd find some way to prove she was a worthy hunter, even if they wouldn't help. When Joe and the men returned, she'd be a better shot and better tracker than when they left. And as soon as Bullet was well enough, she'd be ready.

* * *

Each day seemed to drag past while Joe and the other men were away. Grace duly worked with the women when they needed her, but her mind was not really on the tasks. Now that she was starting to feel better, she took every opportunity to sneak away and start training in earnest on her own. She set up targets and practised her aim with a pistol, her quick draw, and her skills with the Ndeh weapons too. She set traps and checked them each morning like Joe had taught her to. But with each skill she set herself to master, she couldn't help feeling a sense of something missing. Grace had to admit to herself that it was having Joe there to teach her, to encourage and help her … to laugh with her…

She tried to shake the feeling away, even when her thoughts drifted to him as she lay in her *kuugh'a* at night trying to get to sleep. Along with the usual concerns about having nightmares of the trauma she'd been through, she couldn't help worrying about Joe. Was he safe? Was the hunt going to plan? When would he be back?

When the men finally returned a few days later – but after what seemed to Grace like an age – they came bearing two hulking bison. Their hides were thick with dark, bloodstained fur, and even Grace had to admit that bagging such beasts must have been a feat. As the women and children crowded around, cheering and congratulating the hunters, Grace sidled up to Joe. It was a relief to see him back safely, but she was also desperate to continue her training with him. She begged him to begin teaching her more now, while everyone was distracted.

"I'm exhausted." Tired lines ringed Joe's eyes. "Can it wait?"

Grace's shoulders sagged, but she nodded. "All right. I've been waiting so long, another day won't matter…"

"And you missed out on this hunt too." Joe flashed her an understanding smile, and she grinned back. Having been left at the camp all this time, she had forgotten how good it was to have Joe around. He stared at her for a while, a difficult-to-read expression passing over his face.

Perhaps he'd missed her too? "OK, fine," he relented. "I'm still in hunting mode, I guess. Let's go." He stopped, looking down self-consciously. "Oh, let me wash off the bear grease first."

Grace laughed. "You don't have to. I've gotten used to the smell."

Joe smiled. "Why don't you go get your gun while I wash up? Meet me here in a short while."

By the time he returned from the stream, shaking the water from his hair, loaded down with weapons, Grace was waiting, impatient to get started. The rest of the camp had started preparations for a celebratory feast, so no one noticed them slipping down the path into the woods. No one except Tarak.

He shouted at them, his angry words slicing through the air so loudly that he silenced the joyful crowd. Joe spun to face him and the two of them exchanged heated words as the rest of the band stared.

Grace looked between the two of them impatiently, her blood boiling at Tarak's constant intervention. "What is he saying?"

Joe frowned. "It doesn't matter."

"It's about me again, isn't it?"

"And me."

Tarak pinned Grace with a glare and switched to English finally. "You are not Ndeh. Paleface woman should not learn ways of the Ndeh hunter." His face contorted, and he spilled out another torrent of words she didn't understand.

Grace's anger ignited like gunpowder. "You—"

Joe quickly set a hand on her shoulder. "It's not worth it." Then he turned her around and, with one arm around her, led Grace, who was still spluttering, away.

Tarak's taunts followed them down the path.

"Why didn't you let me have my say?" Grace's hands were still clenched into fists and anger simmered in her chest.

"Tarak's anger isn't just about you." Joe sighed. "Today he's even more upset than usual, because it was me who killed one of the bison. His shots went wild."

"So you're the hero?" Grace grinned teasingly, and her anger subsided a little.

"You could say that." Joe suppressed a grin of his own and motioned for her to move down the path. "Enough about me. Come on, let's turn you into a Ndeh warrior."

CHAPTER TWELVE

Joe suggested he start by showing her how to find water if she wasn't near a stream, but Grace declined. "I'd rather learn how to kill something. The way you did with the boar. Something hard to shoot."

Joe shook his head. "You'd be better off learning about survival, like what plants to eat." He gave her a stern glance. "Or not eat."

Grace glared and crossed her arms. "Will you never let me live that down? I won't make that mistake again."

"Yeah, but you'll probably make another."

She gritted her teeth. "Let's not argue. There's too much I need to learn."

Joe opened his pouch. "I found some bullets for your Colt when I was at the mercantile the other day. Now you have no more excuses about not having enough bullets."

Grace bit back a sharp retort and forced herself to thank him, but his kindness weighed on her conscience. One more thing she'd have to pay him back for. She slid some of the bullets into the gun while Joe set up some targets, then came and stood beside her. "So, now let's see what you can do."

Grace's arm felt much steadier than it had last time. She'd done this with Pa; she could do it again and finally show Joe. Taking a deep breath, she fired. The first shot went a bit wide but nicked the edge of the target. The report of the gun threw her back a bit and she tutted under her breath, but waited until the black smoke cleared, then steadied her arm. She gritted her teeth and aimed again.

Almost. Just slightly off centre.

"Hey, that wasn't bad," Joe said.

Hmm, he thought so, did he? Wait until he saw her next few shots. She was just getting warmed up. Her sore arm throbbed and her palms were still a bit tender, but she gripped the gun, took her time aiming … then fired.

Bullseye!

Ha! So what would he think of that? Grace turned and laughed to see Joe's look of surprise.

"Aw, just luck," he said with a wink.

Grace let out a short scoff of indignation, then squeezed

off a few more shots in succession. All of them dead centre or very close.

"Whew." Joe pretended to wipe off his forehead. "Sure glad you weren't aiming at me."

Grace raised an eyebrow. "I could be."

Joe threw up his hands in mock surrender. "No, no, please don't shoot," he said in a falsetto voice. "Besides," he said, returning to his normal voice, "who'd teach you all the other things you need to learn?"

"Right," said Grace. "So now that you know I can shoot, what's next?"

"You know, if you shoot that good, you should do some competitions. Good way to earn money. But you have to learn the Fast Draw."

"What's that?" Competitions and earning money sounded good to Grace. She needed to find some way to support herself – and to pay Joe back. Once she'd taken care of the Guiltless Gang…

Joe holstered his gun. "Watch." His hand hovered above his gun, then he clicked his tongue and in one rapid motion slid the gun out of the holster, tilted his body back, and fired.

"Wow. How do you do that? You didn't even take time to aim."

"It takes practice, but it's a great skill to have."

"Show me," Grace demanded.

Joe spent the next few hours demonstrating the technique.

149

"In a competition you have to keep your hand in a ready position but can't touch the gun until they give the signal. That's why I'm making that clicking noise with my tongue. When I make it, you try."

Grace learned quickly. She wasn't as accurate as when she took her time and aimed, but she was getting the hang of it.

"You're doing great," Joe said, then he added teasingly, "But you'll never be as good as me."

Grace gave his shoulder a gentle shove. "You think so? We'll just see about that—" Then she clapped her hand over her nose. "Ugh, what's that awful smell?"

Joe laughed. "At least I know it's not me this time." He grabbed her arm and pulled her behind a tree. "Watch and you'll see."

A pack of hairy pigs stampeded toward them. No, not pigs – they had tusks.

"Javelina," Joe whispered.

Grace tensed. "Will they attack us?"

Joe shook his head. "Stay still. They have terrible eyesight. Chances are they'll pass right by without seeing us."

The stench grew worse as the animals charged through the clearing, snorting and grunting. Grace pinched her nose shut. Joe waited until the last one had disappeared from sight before stepping out from behind the tree. "They're gone. But javelina aren't usually dangerous, anyhow."

"I remember now. My pa shot a javelina once…" Grace

swallowed hard, remembering her father's triumphant grin as he'd brought it home. "Ma had to cook it all day in a pit, but it tasted good. Like pork."

Joe's jaw tightened. "Some people *do* eat them, but—" he began.

"I just never knew what they looked like – or that they were so stinky!" Grace exclaimed. "I might not have eaten it if I'd known."

"Your pa must have skinned it right away, taken off the musk gland on its back. That's what makes them smell so disgusting." Joe glanced off in the direction the javelina had fled. "He did well to get one though. They're hard to kill because they have such a small kill zone." He shook his head. "Not that you'd ever need to know that."

Grace shivered thinking about getting caught in that snorting pack with their sharp tusks. "But what if they attacked?"

"Don't worry. They won't."

"But what if they did?" Grace persisted. They certainly didn't look harmless.

Joe pursed his lips. "Never let anything go, do ya?" he said wryly, but then continued. "Best way to defend yourself is to get them behind the collar, just above the front leg." He made a circle with his thumbs and forefingers. "They have a spot about that big to hit. But they'll go down right away if they're hit in that kill zone."

151

"What if you miss?"

"They can stay alive for hours. But, like I said, you don't need to worry about all that." Joe motioned for Grace to move ahead of him onto the trail. "We should get back for the feast."

They walked back to the village in companionable silence. Inside, Grace was elated at how well she had done on her first session of training. But she still had to learn how use the bow and arrow, tomahawk, and knife.

She'd need to know everything she could in order to take on Elijah Hale and his gang of murderers.

CHAPTER THIRTEEN

The days began to pass more quickly. Bullet was on the mend, but Cheveyo warned her that he still couldn't be ridden until he was fully healed. Though she was impatient to be off, Grace was surprised at how much the village had come to feel like home.

But this time of day was always hard. A lump rose in Grace's throat as she watched steam rising from cook pots as women bent over the fires. They still reminded her so much of Ma and that last pot of stew. She turned away, but smiled as she saw that Sequoyah was heading toward her. The two of them had become fast friends.

"Are you going into the woods with Joe again?"

Sequoyah asked.

Grace nodded. After she'd confessed to Joe how painful it was to watch the village families eat their meals together, he had suggested they train during mealtimes. He'd bring some food and they'd snack as Grace practised. She'd been grateful he hadn't made a big deal about it, even though she had a feeling the others – Tarak in particular – didn't like him going off instead of eating with them.

A mischievous grin spread across Sequoyah's face. "You know what everyone say about you two? They think you are…" She wrapped her hands around her body and hugged herself tightly, raising her eyebrows.

Grace's cheeks grew hot. "We are *not*. He's teaching me to throw a tomahawk, use a knife, and how to stalk prey, and—"

Sequoyah's smile broadened. "But you like him?" She puckered her lips and made a kissing sound. "You want him to do this?"

"No! Of course not. I just want to learn to survive." And to learn more about how to track, and how to sneak up on the Guiltless Gang without them knowing she was there. She'd come to realize that was the only way she'd manage to take them down. One by one, without them suspecting. But she'd stopped saying it to Joe or the others, because they all just gave her lectures either about how foolish she was, or about how she needed to forgive and let God – or Usen – deal with revenge.

Just then, Joe's voice came from behind her. "Hello,

154

Sequoyah. Ready to go, Grace?"

Grace's whole face flamed. Had he heard Sequoyah's comments? Seen her kissing motions? She didn't want Joe thinking she wished he would kiss her... Or did she? She shook off those thoughts, bidding Sequoyah a rather brusque goodbye.

When hurt flared in her friend's eyes, Grace softened it with a gentle, "I'll see you later."

Sequoyah's face relaxed into a smile. "You two have fun."

"Oh, we will," Joe said breezily. "We always do."

Grace gritted her teeth. Now he'd made it sound like Sequoyah's suspicions were right. But did he mean it...? *Uh, stop it, Grace!*

"Enjoy your meal," she said quickly, waving to Sequoyah and turning to go with Joe.

"Be careful," Sequoyah called.

"I'm always careful," Joe said with a grin. "Grace is the one who has trouble with that—"

"No." Sequoyah caught up with them again and her tone turned low and urgent. "Tarak is much angry. He say over and over, you should not teach a white woman our way." She laid a hand on Joe's arm. "He try to make trouble."

Joe studied her tense face for a moment. "Thanks for the warning, Sequoyah. I'll keep watch."

Sequoyah nodded, but her shoulders remained tense. "I must help with the meal." She scurried away.

155

Joe watched her go, a worried look in his eye.

"Would Tarak try to hurt you?" Grace asked.

Joe sucked on his lower lip, a scowl on his face. "I'm not worried about what he might do to me. I could take him in a fight, unless he gets a group to ambush me – but I don't think he'd go that far. It's you I'm worried about."

"Don't worry about me. I'm not afraid of him." After all, she planned to track down a gang of murderers. Compared to that, one angry Ndeh brave wasn't that scary. "Come on, let's go."

The two of them set off into the woods. First they checked the traps Joe had taught Grace how to set, and along the way he showed her some edible plants. He paused and looked at her – she knew what was coming. "So you won't make the same mistake again."

He made a show of cowering away as she playfully punched him on the arm. They both laughed, but the stubborn part of her was still a little annoyed. Couldn't he let her forget it? She'd been tired and starving. If she hadn't been so upset, she might have been more careful. But the truth was she *hadn't* known the plant was dangerous, and if she planned to survive, she'd need all the knowledge she could get.

Next, Joe had her practise some tracking, a skill Grace enjoyed but she had trouble remaining motionless for what felt like hours. When Joe tracked her, she never heard him approach, but when it was her turn, he always sensed her presence even if she thought she'd been totally silent. But she'd become much more skilled with the weapons. She'd shot a few animals for meals but let Joe take the credit back at camp. She didn't want Tarak to know how fast she was learning.

Now, after making two good kills in a row during their practice, she was bursting with pride at how good she was getting at hunting. Before she could check herself, Grace made the mistake of saying, "I'll soon be ready to take down the Guiltless Gang."

Joe stopped dead and turned to her. "Grace, I thought you'd given up on that? I've been teaching you *survival* skills. Not skills to take anybody down."

Grace stared at the ground, shuffled her feet. "I know … I know you and Cheveyo want me to forgive and forget, but I *can't*. I've tried, but I just can't let this go." She looked up at him. "Can you forget what happened to your dad? If you *knew* who those bandits were, you'd go after them, wouldn't you?"

"I don't know who they are." The flatness of Joe's tone discouraged any more probing. "And the Ndeh taught me to let go of the past."

"But you understand how I feel, don't you?"

"I know what it's like to be lonely even in a crowd. To ache with an emptiness that nothing can touch, that nothing can fill, but—"

"And if you had the chance, wouldn't you want to see your family's murderers hanged?"

When Joe didn't respond, Grace clenched her fists. "Well, I do. And I'll *never* give up until I see every one of them brought to justice."

Disappointment filled Joe's eyes. "I worry about you and this desire for revenge. I hoped staying here would allow you to let go." His voice took on a warning tone. "Be careful about staring into the darkness for too long, Grace. You might lose yourself forever."

Grace kept silent now, but her heart sank. She had been sure he'd understand. The only thing she cared about was her family's honour, and she didn't need any more lectures about forgiveness. She exhaled hard and decided to change the subject.

"What was it like growing up with the Ndeh?" Maybe she'd find a clue to how he could have possibly forgiven his father's killers just from spending time with the tribe.

"I don't remember much of the first few years. They're a blur of anger, sadness, and confusion. I threw myself into learning every skill I could in case I was ever attacked." He looked at Grace. "A lot like you're doing now."

Grace felt a glimmer of hope – maybe he did understand. "You learned well," she said.

"Not as quickly as you. But I was younger. And in pain." Joe tilted his head to one side. "But Cheis treated me like a son, and over time I healed." Moisture glinted in his eyes. "Not that you ever *forget*. But it does get easier with time."

Grace's pain was too fresh, too deep. She wasn't sure it would ever heal.

Joe stared off into the distance and his words sounded dreamy, almost as if he were talking to himself. "I guess my first clear memories are of my initiation into manhood…"

Grace nodded for him to continue.

"Ndeh boys start training when they're small, so I had a lot of catching up to do. We rose before dawn and raced up the mountain, then we jumped into the icy stream." He smiled wryly. "At least, they did. I trailed far behind even the youngest boys."

Grace could picture him as a young boy, struggling to keep up with the others. She smiled.

"But by the time I was 10, I could keep up with the best of them. I even outdistanced Tarak. He never forgave me for that either," he said, shaking his head.

Grace's fists clenched at the mention of Tarak's name. "Seems like he doesn't forgive anyone."

The gaze Joe turned on her pierced straight to her heart, and she hung her head. So maybe Tarak wasn't the only one who couldn't forgive. But at least her anger was justified.

Silence stretched between them until Grace could stand it no longer. "So you became a hunter, a warrior, by running and jumping into the water?"

Joe cleared his throat. "We also learned to use weapons. And they taught us a secret language." When Grace looked at him questioningly, he shook his head. "No, I can't share it with you. It's for men only. Tarak worries that I might tell you, but I won't betray the trust the Ndeh placed in me, not on that."

Grace was curious, but she wouldn't ask Joe to break his vow. "OK. I understand."

"Anyway, that year I made my first raid—"

"A raid?"

"To be a warrior, we had to do four raids on enemy settlements."

"And you did it? Sounds dangerous."

Joe nodded and lifted the leather thong around his neck. A wooden hoop dangled from it, along with four turquoise stones, and a small leather pouch bounced against his chest as he ran it through his fingers. "As you can see, I have my warrior's necklace for strength and protection. And I got my name, Ahote, because I like to wander."

Grace studied him. He seemed so much a part of the Ndeh camp, she wondered if the name Restless One really fit him. "But the Ndeh are your family now?"

Joe was quiet for a moment. "I'm with them, but not of them."

She understood the feeling of distance. Grace hadn't been there as long as he had, but she knew what it felt like to be an outsider. Maybe Joe understood that more than she'd given him credit for. "But the boys who went to war with you, they must be like brothers now?" Except Tarak, perhaps.

"I'm close to most of them." Joe's face grew sad. "But not all of us made it back."

"Parents let their children go, knowing they might die?" Grace was horrified.

"It's a harsh life out there in the wild. If a boy doesn't make it then, he won't survive later."

"But that's awful."

Joe pinned her with a stare. "Is it any more awful than what you're planning to do?"

Grace averted her eyes as they clouded with anger. She didn't want to get in another argument, but she wasn't planning to kill innocent children. The Guiltless Gang were evil men. There was a big difference.

"You know, out there alone for so long, I had a lot of time to think. To face my inner demons. To wrestle with my pain. I came back changed."

Grace glanced back at him. "I guess that makes sense."

"I learned that anger and revenge eat away at you. They rob you of peace."

She sighed. "So everyone's been telling me. Guess I'll have to learn it for myself." Grace picked up a tomahawk.

Joe gave her a knowing look. "Ready for some more practice?"

"Definitely." And ready to stop hearing lectures on forgiveness.

Joe showed her several times, but Grace still struggled to

161

throw with enough strength to get the heavy stone head to fly through the air with the right arc to hit a target. She tried and tried, but instead of getting better, her throws seemed to be getting worse.

"Why don't you take a break and try something else for a while?" Joe suggested.

But Grace was determined to master this. "I'm going to keep going until I get it right."

"Then maybe we need to adjust your grip or follow-through." Joe stepped up behind her. "I'm going to put my hand on your arm and do it with you. Maybe we can figure out what's wrong." He moved close to her back and fitted his arm under hers. The warmth of his body pressed against hers startled Grace so much that she almost dropped the tomahawk, and she went rigid in his arms.

"If you're always this stiff when you're throwing, it's no wonder you miss." Joe's breath against her ear set her pulses racing and shivers sliding down her spine.

"I'm – I'm not always—" Grace drew in a breath and tried to relax.

"Show me how you lift your arm."

Grace's muscles wouldn't cooperate. Her arm lifted jerkily.

Joe chuckled. "You'll have to do it more smoothly than that."

"I know! I'm just … not used to having someone behind me."

"Just relax and pretend I'm not here."

That was impossible, but Grace tried to clear her mind and get into the throw. Still, she let go too early, and the tomahawk plummeted to the ground a few feet in front of them.

Joe sighed.

"I wasn't ready," Grace said defensively.

"I could tell." He released her and went to pick up the tomahawk. "Let's try again."

Though they tried several more times, Grace's body refused to cooperate. With Joe's arm under hers and his body so close, she could barely breathe, let alone concentrate. How could someone who could make her so angry make her feel like this too? And worst of all, Sequoyah's comments kept taunting her. Grace didn't really want Joe to kiss her, did she? Of course not. But she couldn't help wondering what it would feel like to have Joe's arms around her, his lips pressed to hers...

She blushed, and shook the thought from her head. *Focus*, she told herself.

CHAPTER FOURTEEN

The next day, Grace saw Sequoyah heading toward the medicine lodge. Most of the young men had gone off hunting, but once again Joe had refused to let Grace accompany them and try out her skills. Instead, she hurried after Sequoyah, needing to find something to do to distract her from her annoyance at being excluded again. And from her strange new thoughts about Joe...

"Sequoyah, wait," Grace called. "Where are you going?"

Her friend stopped and waited for Grace to catch up. "Cheveyo, he teach me to be a shaman. I learn about healing."

"Cheveyo did a wonderful job healing my arm." Grace held it up. It was still scarred, but much better. "I'd like to see what you're learning. May I watch?"

Sequoyah smiled at Grace's eagerness, but tempered it by warning, "This is sacred. I ask Cheveyo if OK."

When they reached the lodge, Sequoyah talked to Cheveyo in rapid-fire words. At first he shook his head, but Sequoyah's voice turned pleading.

After some argument back and forth, Cheveyo turned to Grace. "You cannot watch."

Disappointment flooded through her. She turned to leave but Sequoyah grasped her arm.

"You stay."

Grace shook her head. "Not if Cheveyo says no."

"He say you cannot not watch. You must *do*. You must learn to heal."

"You mean he's willing to teach me to heal too?"

When Sequoyah nodded, Grace squealed and hugged her. Sequoyah looked surprised at first, then she hugged her back.

"Thank you!" Grace said, looking from one to the other.

Cheveyo's normally stern face split into a grin. "You must work hard."

"I will. I promise," Grace said quickly. She hoped she could learn what ointment he had used to heal her blistered hands. She already knew he had put willow bark on her infected arm. Maybe she could leave sooner if she knew what Bullet needed to heal completely. Having the skills to take care of herself and Bullet would be really important when she set out on her own.

165

Cheveyo sent them out to gather several plants.

Sequoyah hurried along with Grace at her side. "I will show you where zagosti grows."

Grace helped harvest the weed that Sequoyah said made old people's blood flow through them more easily. After they had dug up osha root, they returned to the medicine lodge, where Cheveyo showed them how to grind the osha root with tobacco.

"What is this used for?" Grace asked as she tried to copy Sequoyah's motions with the mortar and pestle.

Cheveyo did not answer but looked to Sequoyah. "Tell Ger-race what this do."

Sequoyah shook her head. "I do not know the English word." Then she smiled. "It is for this." She sneezed, then rubbed under her nose with the back of her hand.

Grace smiled. "A cold? It's for colds."

"No. Cold is this." Sequoyah clasped her arms around her and shivered.

How could Grace explain that *cold* meant two different things? "You are right," Grace said. "This is cold." She repeated Sequoyah's shiver. "But we also say this is a cold." She *achoo*ed.

Sequoyah frowned. "Same word?"

Grace nodded. "That's right."

Sequoya chuckled.

After giving them several tasks, Cheveyo left to see a patient. Sequoyah wrapped some ground herbs in bundles and then turned to Grace with a curious look on her face. "You and Joe *now*…?" She pressing her hands together and opening her large, doe-like eyes wide with a yearning look.

Grace almost choked. "No, no, no." *Of course not!* Why did she keep asking?

"You look at him like this." Again Sequoyah made the wide-eyed look of longing.

"You're mistaken." *Would Sequoyah know that word?* "I mean, you are wrong. I do not like Joe, I told you."

Sequoyah smiled, and the sly look she gave her showed she didn't believe Grace's protests.

Did everyone think she and Joe were…? Were what? Friends? More than friends? Had *Joe* gotten that impression? Just because she got a bit skittish when he touched her, it didn't mean she liked him, did it? Not in the way Sequoyah was implying. All right, that one time she had wondered what it would be like to kiss him, but—

Grace reined in her runaway thoughts. She didn't like Joe in that way. Not at all.

Sequoyah pointed to herself then clasped her hands against her chest. "I tell you the man I like…" she whispered.

"You are … with someone in the tribe?"

Sadness tugged at the corners of Sequoyah's mouth. "No."

"But you like someone. You wish he *was* your beau?" Grace was pretty sure she knew who that was – the young musician Sequoyah had been eyeing at the dance.

"Beau?" Sequoyah considered for a moment. If she didn't understand the word, she obviously understood its meaning. "Yes, yes." The sadness in Sequoyah's eyes changed to suppressed excitement. "It is Dahana."

"You like Dahana." Grace grinned. At least they'd moved off her as the subject.

A sigh was Sequoyah's only reply. After a few moments of silence, Sequoyah spoke again. "It is soon time for me to marry."

"Already? Aren't you too young?"

"Ten moons ago I bleed like a woman. Then we have Sunrise Ceremony. This show everyone I am a woman. When two more moons pass, it is time to marry."

Grace guessed that moons were like months. So Sequoyah had started her menses 10 months ago? Then a year later she'd get married? If the English did it like that, Grace would have been married for three years already. She couldn't imagine it. But for some odd reason she wondered ... if she stayed here, would Joe offer to marry her? She shook the notion out of her head. *What is wrong with me?*

Sequoyah broke into Grace's thoughts. "My father, he say Tarak is good man to marry. But ... but I have great joy when I look at Dahana."

Grace grimaced at the notion of marrying Tarak. "You can't choose who you will marry?"

Sequoyah ducked her head. "I may choose the man I marry.

But my father is great man. Very wise. He know what is best. I will do what he say."

"Have you told him you love Dahana?"

Sequoyah shook her head. "No. I will obey his wishes."

"But you *should* tell him. He loves you very much. He would probably listen and let you marry the person you want."

"That is why I not tell him."

Huh? Grace was confused. "I don't understand. Why not?"

Sequoyah pinched her lips together for a few moments. When she spoke, her words carried the weight of great sadness. "If my father say marry Tarak, he have good reason. He know many things I not know."

"So you don't want to influence his decision?"

"In-flew-ens?"

Having these conversations was hard. How did Grace explain what she meant? She tried to think of simpler words. "You don't want to make him change his mind? To make him think differently?"

"That is so." Sequoyah nodded.

Grace smiled. "Your father... He would be sad to know that you did not follow your heart."

The frown on Sequoyah's brow showed she did not understand. Grace tried again. "Your father would not want you to be sad. You should marry the man you love."

"And you must marry the man *you* love." Sequoyah grinned broadly.

Grace stood and brushed off the back of her skirt, trying not to cringe when her fingers brushed across the deer tails dangling behind. She'd had enough talk about men and marriage. "We need to get back to work, don't we?"

They worked in silence until Sequoyah had to leave to prepare the evening meal. Then Grace wandered off alone. The men had still not returned from the hunt, so Joe wouldn't be around for lessons tonight. Grace felt sad and lonely, but also relieved. All these new feelings tumbling around inside had her off balance.

She drifted off toward the horses – being around Bullet always comforted her. Bullet neighed when he saw her and as he made his way toward her Grace frowned to see that his gait was still uneven. She sat in the field with him, gazing down at the town of Tombstone as darkness fell. She wished she could go hunting with the braves. She needed to practise her skills. But how could she get them to accept her as one of the party? She had to do something to show she had what it took to be a hunter. To prove it not only to Joe and Tarak, but to herself as well.

And then Grace had an idea.

CHAPTER FIFTEEN

Sequoyah eyes widened when Grace exited her *kuugh'a* the next morning with a lance strapped to her back, a knife tucked into the top cuff of her moccasins, and a gun holstered at her side.

"You not come to Cheveyo house with me?"

Grace shook her head. "I have some hunting to do."

Sequoyah wrinkled her nose. "You have bear grease on you?"

Grace nodded.

"But the men leave already. You are too late. You know they not want girls along."

"I know," Grace said tightly. She had watched the men leave at dawn, moving single file into the woods. They hadn't ridden horses, which was why Grace had decided today was the perfect day to execute her own idea. "I have other plans. If Joe comes back, let him know I borrowed his horse. I'll be back before sunset."

Though Sequoyah protested, Grace was adamant. She had to prove to herself and everyone else what she was capable of.

Grace set off in the opposite direction from the one the warriors had taken. She didn't want to take a chance of running into them. If they knew what she was about to do, they'd stop her for sure – but if she was successful, she'd know in her heart that she was ready to track down the Guiltless Gang.

Grace untethered Joe's horse, Paint, and led him out of the enclosure. Joe had told her she was free to ride his horse any time, but if he knew what her plans were, he wouldn't be happy. When she had ridden deep enough into the woods, Grace tied Paint to a tree and set to work.

All morning long, she did everything Joe had taught her. She crawled on her belly with branches in front of her to disguise herself. She lay quiet a short distance from the stream. Although she surprised several woodrats and a rabbit, she shot none of them. Grace was after larger game. Something that would prove to the village that she was a great warrior.

By afternoon, though, she was staring to become discouraged. Perhaps she'd need to settle for a rabbit after all? But just as she was ready to give up, she spotted movement in the distance. Grace crawled slowly toward it, her heart

172

pounding so hard her chest ached. Moving over the rough, rocky ground inch by inch, she managed to get within viewing distance.

Ugh! And smelling distance.

Javelina. All that work for some stinky pigs? Grace had hoped for a deer or an elk, something large to drag back for a feast. But wait. Joe had said they had a small kill zone. If she could hit that and bring back one or two, that would prove she was a good hunter, wouldn't it?

Grace pulled out her gun, steadied her arm on the ground, took aim, and fired. The javelina jumped at the noise and scattered, and the bullet went past the one she'd aimed at.

She leaped to her feet and raced after one, finger on the trigger, hoping for a clear shot, but suddenly she tripped over a tree root and went flying. The gun flew from her hand, hit the ground, and discharged. She ducked, her heart racing, and the bullet clipped the javelina's ear. Enraged, it turned in circles, squealing in pain.

Before she could dive for the gun, the javelina charged toward her, its tusks like spears pointed in her direction. It sped over the ground between them.

Grace froze.

She'd never make it to her gun now. Yanking the knife from her moccasin cuff, she pointed it toward the javelina as it galloped closer and closer. Grace had never been so frightened in her life. Her heart was in her throat. Her hands were slicked

173

with sweat and drops beaded on her forehead and slid down her cheeks, her neck. She had to wait until the boar was close enough to hit … but if she timed it wrong, she was dead.

Joe's words came back to her. *The kill zone. Behind the collar above the front leg.* Grace stood steady, knife at the ready. *Aim for the kill zone.* Timing was everything.

She took a deep breath and sidestepped out of the javelina's path. As it passed, she buried the knife above its foreleg, hoping she'd hit the right spot.

But the javelina kept running.

Had she missed?

Then its legs buckled. It crashed to the ground, snorting and squealing. Grace rushed toward it. Staying clear of the thrashing tusks and legs, she slashed at the spot again, until at last it lay still. Then, panting, she stood over it, shocked and sickened.

But also thrilled.

She'd done it. She'd made her first kill.

Grace sank to the ground a short distance away from the dead javelina until her heart slowed and she could finally draw in a breath. *She'd done it.* Her whole body still trembled with the rush of energy that had shot through her. When she'd composed herself, she stood and forced herself to skin the beast. Her arms shook with the exertion and pent-up emotions as she slid the knife under the hairy hide. She'd helped the women skin game before, but this time she had to be careful to find the stinky gland Joe said was on its back. Not far from the tail, she reached what looked like a nipple. She blew out a relieved breath when it came free with the skin.

She wiped her hands in the grass and picked up her kill. Then she mounted, dug her heels into Paint's side, and started back toward the village triumphantly.

Dusk was already falling by the time she arrived, and the people were assembled for storytelling. As she entered the village, everyone stopped and stared. First at Grace with her blood-spattered hands and clothes, then at the carcass she held up. Faces registered disapproval, disbelief, shock, and fury. She spotted Tarak's face hardening into a mask of rage.

Nearby, Joe sat stunned, staring at her and Paint, his mouth gaping. Then he got up and rushed toward her, still looking shocked. "You killed a javelina?"

Grace grinned. "I remembered what you'd told me about the kill zone. I proved I can hunt."

With a sick expression on his face, Joe gripped her arm and led her away from the staring crowd.

"What's wrong? I thought you'd be proud of me. That everyone would see I could do it."

When they were out of sight of the villagers, Joe turned to her, clenching and unclenching his jaw. "This is my fault. I should have told you—"

"Told me what? What's the matter?" If this wasn't enough, what could she do to prove herself?

175

Joe's eyes held anguish. "The Ndeh never kill javelina. It's taboo."

"What?" Grace stood in shock.

"I should have explained that." Joe winced. "I didn't think you'd ever need to kill one."

Grace gulped back the lump in her throat. Instead of everyone being impressed, she'd done something shameful? "All I wanted to do was prove I could hunt," she whispered.

"Oh, Grace." Joe reached around her shoulders and squeezed her to him reassuringly, but quickly pulled back, the tips of his ears red. "Listen, if you hit the kill zone, that proves you're an amazing hunter. I just wish…" He glanced over his shoulder in the direction of the village.

Inside, shame mingled with a whole wave of sensations coursing through her that Joe's hug had started. Grace stared down at the scuffed toes of her moccasins, trying to sort out her tangled feelings.

Joe lightly touched her chin, pulling her gaze so she turned to face him. "You should still be proud of yourself."

The tenderness in his eyes eased some of the ache in Grace's heart. "You taught me well," she said, blushing. Before she did something foolish, she stepped back and said in a deliberately teasing tone, "Still think I'll never be as good as you?"

Joe laughed. "Guess I'll never live *that* down."

She pointed to the carcass. "What do I do with that?"

He shrugged. "Leave it for the coyotes."

Joe led her to the stream to wash, then walked close beside her as they returned to the village. They had barely exited the woods when Sequoyah rushed up to them. "My father wants you to come to the fire. Everyone is assembled and waiting."

The sickness in Grace's stomach increased. They were going to punish her in front of the whole village. What would they do to her for breaking a taboo?

Joe reached over and squeezed her hand briefly before walking over to join the men. The worried look he shot over his shoulder made her even more fearful. Cheis beckoned to her and, dragging her feet, Grace came over to him.

The imposing Ndeh waited until she stood beside him, then lowered a hand onto her shoulder. His touch seemed gentle, but if she squirmed away would he tighten it, hold her prisoner?

Thinking about being a prisoner tightened the knots of fear in her stomach. She quaked a little.

"We have met and discussed it and decided…" Grace tensed as he leaned toward Cheveyo. When Cheveyo handed him a brand-new bow and a quiver full of arrows, she started shaking even more. Did he plan to shoot her? But he was too close to get off a shot…

Instead Cheis held out the weapons towards her. "For you."

"What? For me?"

"You wish to be brave, do you not?"

Confused, Grace looked up at him. "But … but

the javelina?"

Cheis's eyes swam with the sadness of many seasons. "That is taboo. But your heart it is good and true. You do not try to do harm." He extended the bow and the quiver. "This remind you not to do it again."

"I wouldn't have done it if I'd known…" Grace stammered to a stop.

"Then we speak no more of it." He turned her so she faced the crowd and nodded once, showing them he'd forgiven her. "Someday we tell your story around this fire," he told her.

Joe looked as surprised as she was, but then he beamed at her. All around her, people gazed at her with forgiveness and even with affection. But one person's glance darkened as he looked on. Tarak glared at them all and then stalked away, shaking his head.

Yet despite his glare, she had been accepted by the rest of the Ndeh. For the first time since she'd arrived, they at least did not see her as an outsider, but a true member of the band.

And although they'd never replace her own family – pain stirred in her heart at the thought – she was no longer so alone.

But I can't let myself get too comfortable. I've proved I'm capable now. She nodded to herself. As soon as Bullet was healed, she'd be tracking down a different kind of animal. And she'd succeed, the same way she'd succeeded here.

CHAPTER SIXTEEN

Grace had tumbled into bed exhausted and drifted straight off to sleep. For the first time since that horrible day, her sleep was not haunted by nightmares – but early the next morning, she was roused from her sound sleep by a living one.

Thundering hooves and gunshots.

As Grace stumbled from her *kuugh'a*, waves of soldiers galloped into the camp. Shouting and shooting, they galloped through the village. Women and children scattered, shrieking as a hail of bullets mowed through them. Other soldiers torched each *kuugh'a* they passed. Dried grasses whooshed into flame. All around Grace, the camp was ablaze.

Trapped beside the doorway of her *kuugh'a*, she couldn't

move, couldn't think, as the mob charged around her like a herd of stampeding buffalo, with swords flashing, torches waving.

Thundering hooves. Screams. Gunshots. Flames.

Then behind her an eerie war cry went up, sending shivers down her spine. Ndeh men streamed past her, whooping, their faces decorated with hastily applied paint – red, white, black. Some she recognized by their clothing, but they all looked menacing, frightening, with their faces part one colour, part another. The Ndeh warriors set upon the marauders. Knives flashed. Lances and tomahawks flew. Horses charged, screamed, whinnied. Gunfire rained like hailstones; knives and lances glinted in the sunlight.

Grace froze in horror as a soldier dashed past Sequoyah's *kuugh'a* and tossed a burning stick onto the dried grass, setting it ablaze. Flames licked the roof and black smoke spiralled into the dawn sky.

She screamed. Not again. She couldn't bear to see people she cared about hurt. Never again. She had to stop this horror. Terror propelled Grace into motion. She dashed toward Sequoyah's *kuugh'a*, but none of the family had emerged. She had to save them.

But before she could reach the *kuugh'a*, a knife ripped through in the side wall, shredding the grasses. Sequoyah tumbled out, coughing and choking, followed by her brother. Grace stumbled toward them, but Dahana rushed past Grace to help. He dragged Sequoyah away from the flames and ran back, but Sequoyah's brother had already crawled away from the burning *kuugh'a*. He stumbled to his feet, gulping in deep breaths of air.

As clouds of black smoke drifted their way, Dahana barked something to Sequoyah and pointed toward the trees. Then he grabbed his horse's mane and threw his leg over the mustang's back. Still unsteady on his feet, Sequoyah's brother ran to his own horse. He mounted, and Dahana held out his bow and quiver. Then, grabbing the lance he had strapped to his back, Dahana thrust the point out in front of him and the two of them raced down the hill side by side.

Suddenly, Grace spotted Joe. He was galloping past on Paint, armed with a gun and a tomahawk. He, too, had donned war paint, and she barely recognized him with his face smeared black and red.

"Grace! The woods!" he shouted as he saw her. "Get into the woods. You'll be safer there!"

The woods? Anger and adrenalin surged through her. "Why should I run when I know how to fight?" she shouted. Grace dashed to her *kuugh'a* and grabbed her pistol. She slid her knife in her moccasin cuff, slung the quiver Joe had given her over her shoulder, and grabbed her bow. If only she had Bullet…

Grace rushed out toward the battle but a hand snaked around her neck, dragging her backward against a hard body. Grace kicked and flailed, struggling to get away. A horse thundered by carrying a Ndeh in war paint. A knife flashed, plunged into the soldier's neck, and the soldier collapsed against Grace, knocking her over. She slammed into the ground so hard the breath whooshed from her body. Stunned, she lay pinned under the dead soldier, gasping for air. She pushed and shoved at the corpse, trying to get out from under it, until finally she managed to struggle to her feet.

All around her, Ndeh were yanking soldiers from their horses. Some were locked in hand-to-hand combat, while others scalped fallen soldiers. Tarak already had several scalps dangling from his belt as he savagely attacked a soldier from behind. Surrounding the carnage, homes were blazing. Many *kuugh'a* had collapsed into piles of ashes. Great clouds of choking black smoke hung in the air, and bodies littered the ground – some of them women and children. Familiar faces. Waves of nausea churned Grace's stomach, and her vision blurred. Memories of her family lying crumpled, bloodied, the cabin burning, stopped her in her tracks.

Then Joe's desperate yell penetrated the haze around her. Where was he? Grace scanned the battlefield, searching for him. She finally spotted him and her heart stopped. Two soldiers had dragged him from his horse. He was desperately trying to fight them off, but a third soldier was mounting Paint. Grace raced toward Joe, dodging hooves and slashing swords. But on the hill behind her, Sequoyah screamed. Grace whirled. A soldier was dragging her friend away by her hair.

What should she do? Who should she help? Could she get to either of them in time?

A soldier cantered past leading a pack of horses. One was a palomino.

"BULLET!" Grace screamed.

Bucking and kicking, Bullet fought to free himself. With a vicious jerk of his head, he broke away. But rather than heading toward her, he galloped unsteadily toward the hills.

Her heart sinking, Grace whistled … and to her relief Bullet wheeled and sped back toward her.

CHAPTER SEVENTEEN

Hoping she wouldn't damage Bullet's still-healing legs, Grace mounted and rushed to help Joe. One of the soldiers lay curled on the ground, groaning, but the other had Joe's arms pinned behind him. Yanking her knife from her moccasin without hesitation, Grace plunged it into the man's arm. He screamed and let go of Joe.

Joe reached for his gun and managed to get off a shot, but the soldier behind him rose, sword in hand. In one fluid motion, Grace hurled her tomahawk and the man crumpled.

She reached down a hand, and Joe swung up behind her onto Bullet's back. "You … you saved my life!" he yelled above all the noise.

Grace didn't reply. She turned Bullet and galloped toward the spot where she'd last seen Sequoyah. But she had disappeared. Where was she? Had the man dragged her into the woods? But then, high above them on a rocky outcrop, Grace spotted Dahana kneeling over the body of the soldier who she had seen grab Sequoyah, and her friend stood nearby. Relief coursed through Grace – she was safe.

"Head that way," Joe shouted. He pointed to a riderless horse and Grace raced after it. When they came up alongside it, Joe jumped onto the steed in one smooth movement, then charged back into the fray. Grace followed, shooting at anything in uniform that moved. She didn't shoot to kill – her only thought was to stop the soldiers from harming her friends. She was with the Ndeh now, and any enemy of theirs was an enemy of hers.

Warriors gave guttural war cries; the dying and wounded men on the ground screamed and writhed in agony. To her right, she saw Tarak grab a soldier by the hair and scalp him while the man was still alive. Grace's stomach turned and she almost vomited. All the blood, gore, and mayhem. She wanted to flee, to get away, far, far away from killing, chaos, pain, and suffering. But as long as she could fight, she had to stay and help them. Joe dodged a bullet and Grace ducked as an arrow came flying toward her.

Sabres slashed beside her and she saw Cheis had been knocked from his horse and was wrestling in the mud with a soldier. The man's sabre was covered in blood and he had a fistful of Cheis's hair, dragging him closer to the blade. Cheis kicked and punched, but the man holding him stayed just out of reach. Grace set an arrow in her bow and let it fly. It caught the man in the throat and he choked, grabbing for his neck. Cheis tumbled to the ground, but as the man collapsed, he jumped to his feet, mounted his horse, pulled out his shotgun, and took aim—

Grace took off after Joe again. She worried that Bullet might tire and hoped desperately that she wasn't permanently injuring him. Blood splashed the ground; dead bodies lay all around. Bullet jumped over obstacles, landing heavily on his front feet. He didn't have his usual grace or energy. Should she dismount and send him out to pasture? Or would that only get him captured or killed?

She'd lost sight of Joe. She pulled Bullet to the right as a soldier charged toward her. She got off a shot but her aim was low and the bullet hit him in the thigh. He groaned and grabbed for his leg, toppling from his horse. Should she try to finish him off? But before she could fire again, rough hands dragged her from Bullet's back.

A soldier pinned her to the ground. Grace's hat flew off and her hair tumbled free.

A look of shock crossed the soldier's face. "A white girl? You an Apache lover?" He practically spat the words.

Those seconds were all it took. Bullet reared and his

hooves came crashing down on the man's skull, knocking him sideways.

Grace shook herself free of the soldier's still-grasping hands and remounted. But exhaustion was overtaking her. She and Joe had trained, but she hadn't prepared for hours of gruelling, terrifying combat, and Bullet's sides were heaving. She wanted only to ride away from this place now, from the bloodshed and slaughter, from the ugly memories it brought back…

Joe galloped up beside her. "Are you all right?" he yelled.

Fire and determination coursed through her. "I'll be fine," she insisted, wheeling Bullet to head back into the skirmish.

"Wait!" Joe called. "Come with me." He cantered down a path through the woods.

"Where are we going? What about the others?" They shouldn't be leaving the battle now. Or did he plan to circle around the camp for a surprise attack? Grace turned Bullet and chased after him.

Joe motioned for her to slow. Ahead of them on the path were four mounted soldiers. Without warning, Joe whooped out a war cry and took off. Grace galloped after him. Why didn't he just shoot? Was he so honourable that he had to give them fair warning?

One of the men pivoted his upper body and raised a rifle. Joe's shot hit his outstretched arm and the man tumbled from the horse — and two children in front of him fell.

The horse took off, but Grace understood. These soldiers

had taken the *children* prisoners. The youngsters were bundled in front of them on the horses. Joe couldn't shoot for fear of hurting the young Ndeh.

The other men turned as Grace moved in closer. A bullet whizzed past Joe and he yelped but got off another shot, this one to the head of the first soldier, who was still on the ground. Two other soldiers took off, firing over their shoulders. Joe wove back and forth, the way he'd taught her – a moving target was harder to hit.

But the fourth man hadn't pulled his gun. He was struggling with several ropes he'd attached to the children's belts – the Ndeh put their children in belted tunics so they could pick them up and carry them away from danger – but this man had used the belts to tie the children to his horse.

He was winding the ropes around his pommel when Grace squeezed off her shot – but her gun was empty. All she had left was her knife. She had to get within throwing distance while he was still fumbling with the ropes.

The children had their hands tied behind them and their feet shackled together. He'd tossed them onto the horse like sacks of flour. Fury raced through Grace but she had to take careful aim. If her shot went wild, she could hit one of the children.

If she missed, he'd shoot her.

The man looked up at her approach but didn't appear worried. With her blonde hair streaming in the wind, he probably didn't see her as a threat. Maybe he thought she'd been captured by the Apache and was fleeing in the mêlée. Grace kept her hand on the knife hilt poking out of her moccasin to conceal it. He'd be sorry he underestimated her.

She sidled Bullet close to him. "Help me," she begged. It wasn't hard to put a whimper in her voice.

His grin grew broad. "Sure thing, girlie. You ken come along with us." He jerked a thumb toward his captives. "These ones'll fetch a good price in the Mexican mines, but for you I have better things in mind. Bet your parents will pay a good reward to get back a purty lil thing like you."

"Oh, thank you," Grace gasped out. She pulled Bullet close enough to his horse that she could almost touch him, then whipped the knife from her moccasin and plunged it into his back.

With a strange gurgling sound, he fell from his horse, dragging the two children with him. Grace reached for the reins and pulled his horse to a stop. Then she slashed the ropes from the pommel. The children cried as she dismounted and slit their bonds.

"Stay here," she said. "Hide in the woods." They looked at her blankly with wide, frightened eyes. Did any of them understand English? She tried sign language, pantomiming for them to stay here, and tied Bullet to a tree nearby.

Joe had given chase to the other two soldiers and disappeared around a rocky rise. Grace's pulse thundered faster at the sounds of scuffling and low, nasty arguing coming from that direction. Using the tracking methods he had taught her, she slipped silently up the path and peeked around a large rock. One soldier had Joe pinned in a chokehold. The other lay dead on his back, staring at the sky.

Sneaking up behind the man, Grace smashed the butt of her gun onto his head. She may not have any bullets but it still worked as a weapon.

The man crumpled to the ground, and Joe rolled over and sprang to his feet. He kicked the man in the ribs and used his knife to finish him off.

Grace knelt to cut loose the rest of the children that these men had captured. "Tell them to hide," she told Joe in an urgent voice. "I tried to tell the others, but I'm not sure they understood."

Joe talked rapidly to the oldest of the boys and then gave him a nudge in the direction of the others. The boy responded with a stream of words. Joe made a slashing motion and sent him on his way.

"They should be safe here until the battle's over," Joe said, panting. He shook his head. "Grace… You were amazing. Do you realize you saved my life twice today?"

She nodded. "Makes up for the two times you saved mine. We should…" Her words trailed off. The adrenalin coursing through her veins had drained away, leaving her shaky and exhausted – and hungry. She hadn't had anything to eat because

190

the soldiers arrived at daybreak, and they'd been fighting most of the day. The sun had already passed high overhead and was now headed down.

"Are you all right?" Joe's voice came to her from a distance. "Take a drink." He held out his water pouch.

Grace gulped a few mouthfuls of water. "We have to get back." But she was reluctant to return to the mayhem.

"Where's Bullet?" Joe asked.

"I tied him to a tree down there." Grace pointed farther down the trail. "I'm scared I might have permanently damaged him by riding him before he was ready."

"You'd better ride with me then. We'll come back for him."

Now it was Joe's turn to reach down and help her mount. As they galloped back through the trees, Grace, still a bit dizzy and woozy, sagged against Joe. She soaked in the comfort of his warm body and his strength, but being this close to him also stirred up feelings better forgotten. With a great effort, she angled her body away from his, so their bodies didn't touch. In the heat of the battle, she hadn't had time to think about the strange attraction between them, but now that they were alone? Grace shook off the thought. *Forget about that and concentrate on helping his people.*

* * *

191

When they arrived back at the camp, all was silent except for wailing.

There were no more soldiers in sight. Were they truly gone or were they lying in wait, readying for another attack? Grace scanned the village, the bushes, the woods. Relief mingled with grief at the carnage and the families kneeling beside dead loved ones.

"Grace!" Sequoyah screamed her name and raced toward them. "You are safe. And Joe too." She squeezed her eyes shut and clasped her hands over her heart. "I think you both are dead!"

"We're fine." Joe slid from the horse's back. Like Grace, he kept a wary eye on the nearby woods. "Are the soldiers all gone?"

"Yes – but we have prisoners." Sequoyah pointed to where her father and several other men had five soldiers tied, their backs to Grace.

Joe studied the line of prisoners. "Your father is questioning them?"

Sequoyah nodded. Her fists were clenched by her sides. "They have killed many of our people."

Cheis went down the line one by one. When he got to the last man, he pulled out his tomahawk and brought it down hard. The man crumpled to the ground.

"What—" Horror rooted Grace to the spot.

Joe laid a hand on her arm. "Don't watch." He took her by

the shoulders and turned her around gently.

"B-but those men are prisoners. It looked like they answered his questions. Why? Why is he doing that?"

"You have to understand. All these soldiers will be killed."

Grace couldn't believe what she was hearing. "But I thought Ndeh believed in peace? Today they've all turned into bloodthirsty warriors." After everything they'd said, it was almost as if the war paint on their faces had changed them into savage creatures.

"It may seem so to you, but they have their reasons," Joe said. "Those soldiers came months ago to take the Ndeh to a reservation. Cheis refused. The soldiers agreed to let the band live free if Cheis sent a group of his warriors to a meeting to sign a peace treaty. In good faith, eight of our best warriors set off. The soldiers ambushed them. Killed them in cold blood."

Sequoyah broke in. "My father take life of the man that kill his brother."

"The other men will each avenge the death of a family member," Joe explained.

Grace felt sick to her stomach. So much killing, bloodshed, and death. And today she'd done her share.

But how could she criticize Cheis when she, too, wanted revenge?

She turned to Joe. "You all told me not to seek vengeance. Why? When you do the same?"

"It's not easy to understand, but the Ndeh do not seek

revenge the way you do – with hatred in their hearts. They seek only justice. Blood for blood."

"So do I," Grace burst out.

Joe shook his head. "I have seen a bloodthirsty look in your eyes that scares me. I don't think you have the same peace with circumstances as the Ndeh do. And they are disciplined in their vengeance, not wild and desperate."

"At least I'm not out scalping people," she said, her teeth clenched.

"True. But you would if you could." He tilted her chin again so he could look into her eyes.

Grace jerked her head away and muttered, "The Guiltless Gang deserve it. Every last one of them."

"Maybe so. But you'd be better off letting the law take care of them."

"The sheriff, you mean?" Grace projected disdain into her words.

"You know there are others who aren't as easily bought. The deputy? He has a reputation for honesty."

"I've heard that. But if he really is honest, how can he work for Behan?"

Joe shook his head. "I wondered that too. But he's new and naive. Perhaps he doesn't yet realize Behan's crooked."

"If he can't see something that obvious, how much good will he be?" Grace said, frowning.

I have to get out of here, she thought angrily.

But then the thought of leaving Joe and the village to set off on her mission twisted Grace's stomach and constricted her chest. How could she leave these people after she'd fought alongside them? But she wanted justice, just like they clearly did.

Like Joe, she might be with the Ndeh but she was not *of* them. Yet she knew now that, wherever she went in the future, she would always keep them and their teachings close to her heart.

She would evaluate her actions and choices by a code of honour.

CHAPTER EIGHTEEN

The wailing all around the camp grew stronger as the people painted their loved ones' faces red and wrapped them in fur robes.

As they walked through the burned-out village to her *kuugh'a*, Joe leaned close to Grace. "The Ndeh believe the dead turn into ghosts who are jealous of the living. So they bury them in caves far from the camp. It must be done before nightfall. I'll join them, but you should stay here and rest."

Grace shook her head. "I'm coming with you."

The grieving faces, slumped shoulders, bent backs reminded her of burying her family alone. Something wouldn't let her go back on her own and rest while they buried their dead. So many of the dead were people she had known or recognized.

"You don't have to, you know."

"I want to." It was the least she could do after all they'd done for her.

The admiration in Joe's eyes warmed her heart.

"All right," he said. "But you should eat something before you go. I don't want you fainting along the way."

Grace rolled her eyes and ducked into her *kuugh'a*, returning with some pemmican that she pointedly shared with Joe. "Don't want *you* fainting either."

As they moved back through the mourning camp, Sequoyah came over and joined them, her face filled with pain. She pointed to Dahana, who was kneeling beside the bodies of two men. "Dahana's father. And his older brother," she whispered.

Poor Dahana. Grace laid a hand on Sequoyah's arm. "Is everyone in your family safe?"

"I … I do not know. We have not seen my brother. My father fears they took him prisoner." She motioned toward Cheis, who was frantically searching the battlefield, digging through piles of debris, turning over still-smoking mounds of ashes.

Sequoyah sucked in a sharp breath as her father rolled a dead horse off a body trapped beneath. They all watched as he bent down and stared for a moment, then straightened up, his face drained of blood.

"I think … I think Father found him…" Sequoyah

197

whimpered. Tears flowed down her cheeks.

Grace wrapped her arms around her friend. After a few moments, Sequoyah lifted her head. "I must go help Father." Beside them several women stood huddled in a group, wailing uncontrollably. Sequoyah turned to them with pity in her eyes. "They, too, have suffered great loss. The soldiers stole their children. They sell them as slaves."

The children. Grace had forgotten all about the children. *And Bullet...*

"Where's Joe?" she said quickly.

Sequoyah pointed toward a group of people gathered beside the charred remains of a *kuugh'a*. "He help there."

"Joe!" Grace raced over to him. "The children. I need you to help me bring them back."

"OK. Hold on just a moment," he said. Joe's face was a mask of pain as he laid a hand on the shoulder of the boy he'd been kneeling beside and said a few words that Grace couldn't understand. Then he stood and went over to grab Paint's reins, but she could see he was holding his other arm close to his body.

"Are you hurt?"

"It's not bad. It can wait until we return." Joe motioned to Paint. "Hop on. I'll get on behind."

Grace eyed him with concern but didn't argue. She mounted Paint and the two of them tore off into the woods.

When Joe called softly, the children came out from behind

trees or boulders. Some crawled from the underbrush. He talked to them quietly while Grace went over and untied Bullet, who took several hobbling steps toward her and snorted.

"I'd better not ride him," she said, her face tight with concern. "It looks like he's lame."

"Get Cheveyo to look at him when we get back," Joe said, touching her shoulder reassuringly. "He'll probably be all right. I bet he just needs a few more days' rest."

Tears burned behind Grace's eyes. A few days she didn't have. She'd been waiting and waiting to get on the trail, and now she'd probably set herself back several more days.

Joe waited until she had Bullet's reins, then he said, "I'm going to ride back to camp now to help." His voice lowered. "That young boy I was speaking to lost both his parents. He's on his own now, and he'll need help with the burial." They exchanged looks. Another orphan. Joe took a deep breath. "But I told the children to walk back with you. They'll listen."

Many of the children were the ones who had touched her skin and hair the first time she walked through the village. Some of them still followed her or watched her from a distance every day, but now they hung back.

"Can you tell them not to be afraid?" Grace asked.

Joe murmured a few words and the oldest boy shepherded all of the children into a close group. Then he took his place at the end of the line.

With a quick wave, Joe rode off, but Grace was troubled

to see that he was still cradling his left arm close to his chest. She'd have to check his arm when she got back.

Grace led the children back toward the camp, but when she emerged from the woods with the youngsters following single file behind her, sudden shrieks broke out amidst the wailing. As the people saw her coming toward them from the trees, she was shocked that instead of running toward their children, mothers ran the opposite way. Grace whirled around. Had soldiers followed them?

"Grace, wait there!" Joe shouted over to her. Then in a loud voice, so everyone in the camp could hear him, he spoke rapidly in Ndeh and pointed at her. Grace stood next to Bullet, confused. What was he saying?

Sequoyah rushed toward her and hugged her. "You do a much brave thing. You save all the children."

Within moments, mothers surrounded her, hugging their children and patting Grace's arm. Still very puzzled, she waited for Joe to reach her.

"What happened? Why were they so afraid?"

Joe grinned at her. "You are the hero of the day. I told them how you rescued the children."

"And conveniently left out your part?"

He shrugged. "I told them you saved me too. Which you did."

Grace swatted at him. Why was he being so generous? "We need to tell them the truth."

"Some other time," Joe said. "They needed this bit of joy amidst all the sadness."

Grace nodded, but she was still curious. "I don't understand why everyone ran the other way when I got here."

Joe looked around him at the women hugging their children. "Just Ndeh superstition. They thought their children were dead and that you were leading their ghosts back to haunt them."

"Oh. Really?"

"Yeah, like I told you. They have a real fear of ghosts." He smiled wryly at her for a moment, but then his face fell. "Well, now that you're back and the children are safe, they can start the funeral procession. It's getting close to sunset so we have to hurry."

Cheis called to the people, and everyone started off in a long, solemn parade. Several young boys led a group of riderless horses, and when they found a cave large enough for all the dead, they piled the bodies inside. Then, much to Grace's shock, they pulled out their guns and shot the horses.

Grace screamed as the first bullets rang out, but Joe grabbed her arms and pulled her aside.

"Wh-what are they doing? Hasn't there been enough killing?" Her voice was high and shaky but Joe squeezed her arm, leaving his hand resting there as he spoke. "It's… This is their custom. They send the horses to the afterworld with their owners. They won't leave anything around that will attract the ghosts to come back."

"But that's barbaric!"

"Grace, this is their custom. You have to respect it."

She didn't know what to say. So much death, so much killing. So much sorrow. It was overwhelming. As another gunshot rang through the air, she jumped and instinctively pushed her face against Joe's chest, covering her ears and squeezing her eyes shut as tears stung her eyelids. But it didn't do any good. As each bullet was fired, it was as if it hit her in the gut. She felt Joe reach around her, tentatively at first, but then his arms wrapped more tightly, protectively. She breathed him in more deeply, and as she did, she admitted it to herself. There was a feeling of safety, security here in Joe's arms – a feeling she hadn't had at all since she'd left her family buried in the ground.

But she couldn't stay here.

She couldn't let herself get attached to him. If she did, she'd never be able to leave.

Grace forced herself to remember her parents, her mission. She pushed away from Joe's chest and he made a low grunt, like he didn't want to let go. Grace bit her lip and looked up at him, but as he unfolded her from his arms, he winced.

His arm. She'd forgotten about his arm. Grace caught his hand before he could draw it back. "Let me see."

"It'll be fine."

Grace ignored him and turned his arm slightly to see the

blackened spot on his sleeve. "That's from a bullet. Were you hit?"

"Nah. It only grazed me."

Grace leaned closer. "Grazed you? You're bleeding. Look at this sleeve." Gently she worked it up his arm to expose a flesh wound. "You're lucky it didn't penetrate. Cheveyo was teaching me healing. I think I know what to do."

"Hush," Joe whispered. "When we get back." The weeping and wailing increased as Cheveyo said prayers, and then finally it was over.

As everyone turned to go, Joe leaned close, his voice low. "One other thing. Never, ever say the names of the dead. They believe it will bring back the ghosts."

Grace nodded.

They all trudged back in silence, a great heavy weight bowing every back. No family had remained untouched. When they reached the village, several people dipped branches into the fire and carried the burning sticks toward some of the wickiups. Many had already been burned to the ground.

"What are they doing now?" Grace's voice was sharp.

"Shh. It's part of the ceremony. They burn the homes of the dead and all their possessions. Like the horses, it'll keep the ghosts from returning."

As flames engulfed the first house, Grace cracked. Memories of the cabin aflame, the chaos of the morning, and all the losses built inside her chest until she was screaming uncontrollably, but her cries were drowned by the other voices of mourning, the weeping and wailing.

"Grace … Grace, stop…" Through her tears she could see him staring at her, concern etched on his face.

"I … I can't…"

She let Joe slip an arm around her and lead her away to the pasture.

Grace slumped to the ground, still sobbing. He sat down silently beside her, resting one hand on her shoulder as it heaved up and down. Eventually she quieted, and he slipped the arm around her shoulder without saying a word. Like before, he just stayed with her in silence. A silence that spoke of his empathy and understanding.

When her weeping finally ceased, Grace closed her eyes and slumped against a tree, exhausted. The tears had cleansed away some of the poison she'd been holding inside, but now tiredness seeped through her, making her want to drift off to sleep.

Joe leaned against the trunk beside her and finally spoke. "Grace?"

"Umm?" She could barely form the sound.

"At my mother's funeral, I remember the preacher talking about how there is no death, only a change of worlds. And that the dead live on in the hearts of those left behind." He spoke hesitantly. "I know it's not what the Ndeh believe but … I often picture my parents here with me. It helps to ease the ache of missing them."

Grace wasn't sure anything would ever ease that ache, but thinking of Daniel and Pa breaking horses in another world brought a lump to her throat. A longing to see them again. To see Ma's smile. Abby toddling, arms open wide to be picked up. And Zeke... She choked back more tears. Joe reached for hand and held it tightly. She wound her fingers between his, clinging to him for comfort, drawing strength from his touch. They sat there in the darkness and Grace let fleeting memories fill the gaping hole in her heart.

Joe's fingers stroked her palms slowly and Grace tried not to let that strange tingling undermine the comfort he was offering, but she knew. Something had changed between them. She'd sensed it ever since the day he stepped behind her to help her throw the tomahawk.

Grace willed herself not to respond to his touch, not to let the sparks flowing through her hands and up her arm make her shiver.

But it didn't work.

CHAPTER NINETEEN

The next morning when Grace awoke and emerged from her *kuugh'a*, she was startled to see everyone packing their belongings onto horses and dogs. She tried to orient herself, and vaguely remembered having come back to the camp with Joe later that night.

She jumped as he came up behind her. "So, you're finally awake."

"Uh … how's your arm?"

"Much better, thanks to your ministrations last night. Cheveyo taught you well." He reached out as though to smooth her wayward morning hair, but then pulled his hand away, looking embarrassed.

Grace blushed. "It's nothing. I didn't have time to learn much. I watched what he did to my arm and just tried it on yours. I … I'm glad it's working." She gestured toward the village. "What's going on?"

"We're moving camp. Those soldiers who attacked us won't accept defeat. They'll be back with reinforcements. The Ndeh can't stay here."

She shook her head. "That's so unfair."

"Well, they're used to moving. And for them, it's better to move from a place of such great sorrow." His eyes met hers and she was sure his expression mirrored her own. That quiet desperation that said no matter how many moves you make, you can never run from sorrow. You always carry it with you. Even if Joe had done something different with his grief than she'd done with hers, they both bore the inner scars.

For Grace, easing some of the gut-deep pain meant taking revenge – the way the Ndeh had done yesterday. The way she planned to do. Seeing justice done, an eye for an eye, a tooth for a tooth. Or blood for blood, as Joe said yesterday. It all meant the same thing to her. Someone needed to pay. And she couldn't rest until they had.

The people travelled most of the day in heavy silence, Cheis in the lead. Several times he stopped and examined the ground, reaching down to sift the dirt between his fingers. Then he turned in a circle, slowly in each direction. But each time he shook his head, and they moved on. Finally, when the sun was high overhead, he came to a halt. Trees grew near the stream, a cliff rose high behind them, offering natural protection. He turned, rubbed the dirt through his fingers, and gestured. This was where they would set up camp. He and group of men spoke together for a few moments, then they set to work cutting saplings. The women erected the wickiups. This time Grace worked on her own *kuugh'a*, with Joe's help. She was relieved that they could stop walking and rest for a while. She needed to regroup, regather her strength for what was ahead.

"You're doing women's work," she teased as Joe set up the frame and tied the poles into a dome shape. He didn't smile.

"Look around. Other men are helping. At times like this, everyone pitches in. So many people have lost family members."

Grace swallowed the lump in her throat as she realized how many people were missing. The Ndeh had always been gentle and tender with the children since Grace had arrived, but now they were even more so. Seeing the loving glances, tender pats, and frequent hugs made the gaping hole in Grace's heart grow wider.

As soon as the *kuugh'a* was finished, Grace dropped her bundle inside and went to find Bullet. He came when she whistled, and she was amazed to see him trotting toward her with hardly a trace of unevenness in his gait.

Grace flung her arms around his neck. "You're doing better!" She'd been so afraid yesterday's battle had crippled him for good. Instead Bullet seemed frisky, almost back to his usual lively self. Cheveyo must have worked his magic on the horse again.

She stepped back and looked him over closely. "Are you all right?"

Bullet threw back his head and tossed his mane. Then he lowered his neck and nudged her with his nose.

"Is that a yes? You want to go for a ride?" When he turned his liquid eyes to her and looked into hers, Grace smiled. "A ride it is." She hopped onto his back and walked him from the brush enclosure.

Bullet flicked his tail as if impatient with the slow pace, so once they reached the mountain trail Grace gave him his head. Bullet broke into a trot, and soon he was cantering. As the wind whipped past her face, she gave a joyful whoop. Bullet was well again.

Together they rode away from the camp. Away from the sorrow. Away from the past. Up high in the mountains, until she could breathe again. If only she could keep on riding and never look back. But before she left to track down the Guiltless Gang, she knew she had to return to say goodbye properly and thank everyone, and to gather her belongings. They could leave tomorrow at daybreak.

And yet instead of the decision bringing her joy, Grace swallowed the lump that rose in her throat. It would be painful to leave the village … and especially Joe. But she had a mission, and Bullet was well enough now to go.

When she arrived back at camp, to her surprise Cheis called her to his *kuugh'a*. Did he know of her plans already? Though she was eager to begin preparations for her departure, she couldn't deny his request.

Grace ducked into the wickiup, surprised to see how much the inside looked like his previous home. Baskets lined the same walls. Even the strips of meat hung from the ceiling. It seemed he had replaced everything that had burned in the fire – but new lines of sadness and pain were etched around his mouth and eyes; he had aged greatly in the past two days. Grace's heart went out to him. She, too, knew that agony.

Sequoyah and Joe were seated by the fire. So were several of the men who met for council meetings. Cheis nodded toward Grace. "My words are not always right. Joe may need to say what I cannot." He spoke haltingly. "Yesterday you were brave. Very brave. You fought for our people, you saved our children. Words are not enough to thank you." He paused, looking at her closely, then motioned to the deerskin skullcap that fitted over his scalp with several feathers on the top. "We will not give you warrior's headdress. But we will honour you with this." He brought out a beaded headband and tied it around Grace's forehead.

Then, with Joe translating, Cheis said, "My daughter, you are now flesh of our flesh and bone of our bone. Yesterday you were officially taken into the Ndeh Nation. And today we name you Dyami, meaning 'Eagle'. You are one of us." He held up six eagle feathers. "An eagle feather is a sign that you are acknowledged with gratitude, with love, and with ultimate respect. Draw wisdom from the eagle, the master of the sky. It possesses courage and is a messenger from the Great Spirit. You, too, have that courage."

Grace choked back tears as Cheis placed the six eagle feathers in the headband, one by one. She was now a part of them, accepted and loved. Leaving was going to be harder than she ever imagined.

Sequoyah rushed over and hugged Grace, her own eyes gleaming with tears. "Now we are sisters."

Grace hugged her back, but inside her heart twisted. She *had* a sister. No one could take Abby's place. But her true sister was dead. Her whole family was, and she couldn't risk opening her heart that way to anyone else again.

But doubt warred with her need to be loved, and confusion clouded her mind. All Grace wanted was to run away and hide. She didn't want to feel any ties to others. Ties only brought pain and heartache – but the harder she fought, it seemed, the tighter she was tied to those around her.

Tears stung her eyes as she thought of her family and the promise she'd made to get revenge. Surely the Ndeh would understand that she couldn't stay with them? She'd watched them take their own revenge yesterday. No matter *how* close she'd become to all of them and to Joe, she had to strike out on her own tomorrow.

She felt like a fraud, pretending her tears were tears of joy when her heart was breaking. But yesterday she'd proved herself in battle, and she'd learned she could kill. No matter what Joe said, she needed to be able to do that at a moment's notice if she had to. She was ready to take on the Guiltless Gang.

As soon as she could slip out without seeming ungracious, Grace raced back to the meadow to find Bullet. He came running when she whistled, and she patted him and leaned her head against his neck, breathing in the comforting warmth of his horsey smell. Maybe she shouldn't say goodbye at all? Maybe it would be too hard?

"Grace?"

She knew it was Joe. The tenderness and understanding in his tone brought fresh tears to her eyes. When she turned, his tender smile almost made her reconsider her decision to leave altogether.

"I'm so proud of you. Six eagle feathers?" He walked over and touched the headband with one finger. "I said I'd teach you to be a Ndeh warrior, but I never dreamed—" He swallowed hard. "You were unbelievable."

"So were you." Grace looked down at the moccasin toe she was circling in the dirt. Her throat clogged with sadness. She struggled to say the words she needed to say, to tell him she was leaving. But the words wouldn't come.

"What's the matter?" Joe reached out a finger and tilted her chin up to study her face. But when their gazes met and locked, he sucked in a breath.

Grace's heart stuttered to a stop. For one quiet moment they stared deep into each other's eyes, but then Joe exhaled a little – she could feel his breath on her face as he moved closer, his finger still under her chin. She was torn between closing her eyes or keeping them open, but at the last minute she squeezed them shut and waited with breathless anticipation. Waiting for the touch of his lips on hers. Waiting, waiting…

But the kiss never came.

Instead Joe sighed and rested his forehead against hers for a moment and smoothed a hand down the back of her loose hair.

Grace's eyelids flew open and she saw that his gaze was on the ground, his cheeks flushed. He released her and backed away, mumbling a quick good night. Awkward and embarrassed, Grace stammered out a goodbye, staring as he took off down the hill.

She stood where she was, dazed, hurt, and uncertain. She'd been bubbling inside when Joe took her in his arms. She'd never felt such excitement, anticipation, such an overwhelming, inexplicable feeling … and then to have her hopes crushed?

Grace ran her finger over her lips. What would it feel like

to be kissed?

What it would feel like with Joe?

If she left tomorrow, she might never know.

CHAPTER TWENTY

Alone in her *kuugh'a*, Grace lay curled under the buffalo skin. She smoothed her hands across it, dreaming of the way Joe had stroked her hair. She ran a finger over her lips again, soft as a butterfly caress. Would this be what it felt like to have Joe's lips touch hers? Grace drifted off to sleep with thoughts of him holding her close…

The next morning when Grace got up, the first person she saw was Joe. He glanced at her, but didn't say a word. He just turned and headed down to the stream. Didn't he see her? Grace's cheeks burned. Maybe he'd realized last night that he'd be making a big mistake in almost kissing her? After all, he'd pulled away so quickly, and now he couldn't turn his back on her quickly enough this morning. It looked as if their easy companionship was gone, and instead awkwardness was driving a wedge between them. Part of Grace wished none of that had ever happened last night so they could go back to their easy, joking relationship. But the other part of her desperately wanted to see what that kiss would have been like…

It doesn't matter, she told herself. She'd decided – today was her last day here.

But she couldn't help staring at Joe's retreating figure, admiring the muscles rippling on his back, his confident stance, his—

"Grace?" Sequoyah's soft voice behind her made her jump.

Grace turned around quickly, trying to still the rapid beating of her heart. "You scared me!"

Sequoyah looked chagrined. "Oh, I am much sorry." Then her apologetic look turned to one of curiosity. "You and Joe not talk?" she asked, glancing in the direction where he had gone.

Grace frowned. She didn't want to get into a conversation about Joe. She didn't want to think about him – she needed to concentrate on preparing for her journey. Away from here. Away from him.

But before she could say a word, Sequoyah clutched her arm. "Do not fight with Joe. He a good man."

That got Grace right in the gut.

"We aren't fighting. We're—" But Grace had no words to describe the awkwardness that had come between them.

Sequoyah laughed. "OK. You not fight. You want to … kiss?"

"Absolutely not." Grace made her words as firm as her resolve not to think of Joe again with longing.

But Sequoyah's expression became dreamy. "I want to kiss Dahana." A deep sigh escaped from her. "I dream of what it feel like. My friend Sky say it is like floating in clouds."

When Grace didn't respond, she said, "Maybe you know this feeling already?"

"No!" Grace burst out, but then her voice softened. "I … I wish I did…" Then before she knew what was happening, the story of last night and her pain flowed out.

Sequoyah listened intently. Perhaps she only understood half of what Grace was saying, because the words tumbled over themselves in the haste to escape, to get out of her mind. She poured out her frustration, anger, uncertainty, and humiliation.

"Tell Joe," Sequoyah suggested. "*You* could kiss *him*."

Grace shook her head. "I could never do that."

"It is not good to hold in feelings. Not anger. Not love." She nodded toward a shrivelled plant. "You hold bad feelings in here" – Sequoyah patted her chest – "that is what happen to you."

Grace nodded, but she knew she could never tell Joe her real feelings. It would be hard enough to leave Sequoyah and

217

the others who had become such an important part of her life. But parting with Joe would be even more painful now.

Grace said a hasty goodbye to Sequoyah, using the excuse that she needed to care for Bullet. She hurried uphill to where the horses grazed, and Bullet galloped toward her before she could even pucker up her lips to whistle. His gait looked even better today. She only wished inner wounds healed as rapidly.

"Today's the day," she whispered as she stroked Bullet's neck and combed her fingers through his mane. She could leave now, grab her things and go – but something held her back. In spite of everything, she was reluctant to go without seeing Joe one last time. He was only going to the stream for a wash so she knew he'd be back shortly. She wished she had something to give him, something he'd remember her by. And whatever it took, someday she'd pay him back for all his kindness – for the pouch of silver, for saving her life, and for teaching her to shoot, track, and use Ndeh weapons. She owed him so much.

Sequoyah deserved a gift as well. But she had nothing to give.

With a heavy heart, Grace headed back to her *kuugh'a* to pack her belongings and wait for Joe, but just as she did, Sequoyah rushed toward her.

"There you are. My father want to speak to you. Joe is with him, but he want you too."

Grace sighed, but followed Sequoyah to her father's *kuugh'a* and ducked inside. Her eyes struggled to adjust to the semi-darkness inside. Sequoyah had draped buffalo hides over the exterior of the *kuugh'a*, which did not allow much sunlight to penetrate the grass walls, and Grace could barely make out Joe's form on the other side of the fire. She was puzzled – Cheis had already given her the headdress; surely they couldn't have any more honours?

"Welcome, Dyami," Cheis said, nodding toward her. "I have a much big favour to ask. We have lost so much in the fire…" He bowed his head and remained silent for a moment. Grace glanced at Joe, whose head was also bowed. Was he trying to avoid looking at her? At last Cheis looked up and his gaze fell first on Joe, then Grace. "We need help," he began. He peered at them anxiously as if to gauge their reaction.

Joe didn't hesitate. "Whatever it is, I'll do it."

"We need supplies," Cheis said. "But we cannot ride into town."

"The soldiers will ambush you." Joe's tone contained barely concealed anger.

"This is true. So I ask that you two go. They not stop you."

Grace opened her mouth to protest, frustrated that this would delay her even further, but a frown from Joe stopped her. She sat in sullen silence to hear Cheis out, but she didn't see why Joe couldn't go on his own. They didn't need her, did they? Though a part of her still couldn't help wanting to assist them one last time. Perhaps that could be her gift?

Cheis glanced again from one to the other, as though he

knew something. "It will take two of you to carry all that we need," he said pointedly.

Joe jumped to his feet. "We will get ready."

Grace stood more reluctantly. She didn't want to ride with Joe, not with the way things were between them. She didn't want to take off in the opposite direction of the Guiltless Gang. And most of all, she didn't want to go back to Tombstone. The place that reminded her of the worst nightmare of her life, where nobody wanted to help her. The place where the sheriff wanted to lock her up and people wanted to shoot Bullet. But how *could* she say no to Cheis's request? The Ndeh had taken her in, fed her, clothed her, given her shelter, helped her heal. She couldn't refuse, no matter how difficult it was for her.

As she stepped outside into the sunlight, Grace blew out an exasperated breath, remembering how long it had taken her to get up the mountain from Tombstone. She dreaded the long trek there and back. But as Joe too emerged, the look of disappointment he shot at her made her feel guilty.

He shook his head. "After all the Ndeh have done for you, you can't even give them one day of your time?"

"One day?" Grace exclaimed. "We'll be gone for days, Joe."

"It's a half-day's ride at most," he muttered. "We'll be back by nightfall."

Was he joking? "But it took me more than a week to get here."

"I'm not surprised." Joe's voice was gruff. "You didn't know much about surviving in the wilderness then. You probably went around in circles."

Maybe she had, but there was no call for him to be so dismissive. "I'll go saddle Bullet." Grace stalked off.

A short while later, the two of them set off down the mountain, Joe in the lead. Reluctantly Grace reined Bullet in behind Paint. After they made it through the steep, narrow passes, Joe slowed a bit and kept pace beside her. Several times he looked as if he were going to speak, but then he snapped his mouth shut into a thin line, his lips pressed together as if holding back words that wanted to escape. The ride turned into pounding hooves, puffs of dust, relentless heat, and even more relentless silence.

Finally, Joe sighed hard, his brow furrowed and his lips twisted, but his eyes told her that maybe – just maybe – he was as mixed up as she was. That she wasn't just imagining something between them. Strange as it seemed, that idea sparked a little hope in her heart.

"Grace," he said at last, his voice husky. "I … I'm sorry about last night."

"Nothing to be sorry about." Grace tried to make her words sound flippant, neutral.

"I didn't mean to hurt you."

She swallowed. "Hurt me?"

"Yes, it's just that … I, well—" His next words came out in such a rush that Grace could barely make sense of them.

221

"I'm mixed up right now… I mean, I have these feelings when I'm around you that I don't know how to express, y'know, what to do with them. I just, whenever I'm with you…" He tailed off, not seeming to know what else to say.

Grace's heart leaped. So he wasn't as indifferent as he'd seemed this morning? But the thrill she felt bursting in her chest at what he was trying to say soon shrank. She couldn't encourage him. If they got too close, she'd never be able to leave.

Hesitantly, she said, "I'm mixed up too. I only wanted to be friends, but things have changed. But I … I don't want things to be strained between us." She sighed. "I just wish we could go back to the way things were before."

Joe looked hurt, but he seemed to be trying to conceal it. "Oh. Well, I'll be honest," he confessed. "I've had these feelings for a while. I've tried hiding them but I guess that isn't working."

"Can't we … can't we just stay friends?" Grace asked hopefully. She could hardly believe she was saying it. Deep down, she knew that she *didn't* want to just be friends.

Joe sighed. "Maybe that would be best."

Now his rapid response hurt *Grace's* feelings. She'd hoped he'd protest or…

Or what?

* * *

The closer they got to Tombstone, the more nervous Grace got. Her jaw clenched and she clutched the reins more tightly. "Joe?" Grace slowed Bullet. "I'm worried about going back into town."

He chuckled. "Don't worry. No one will recognize you. You look so different cleaned up."

Grace bristled. "I couldn't help the way I looked then. I'd just—" She swallowed hard.

Joe looked over at her and his face fell. "Oh, I'm sorry. I didn't mean it that way." A flush crept up Joe's neck and splashed across his cheeks. "I was just trying to say, um, that you look good now."

That was a compliment? Now it was Grace's turn to be embarrassed. "Thank you," she mumbled. They rode in silence for a few minutes, avoiding each other's eyes. Finally, Grace broke the silence. "Joe?"

"Yeah?" He kept his gaze on the trail in front of them.

Grace had to know. "Did you mean what you said about me looking so different that no will recognize me?"

"Yeah. From then to now? You've … you've really changed, Grace. Inside and out."

Grace smiled at him. "But they'll recognize Bullet."

"Can't miss such a good-looking palomino, that's for sure."

"There's something I didn't tell you," she said. "Something that happened after you left town that day."

Grace explained about the threats in the stable. "I'm worried

223

that someone from the gang or the sheriff might 'accidentally' shoot Bullet." She clenched her jaw angrily. "Or me."

Joe straightened in the saddle, his jaws working. His voice, when it came, was low and hard. "No one's going to hurt either of you. They'll have to go through me first."

Though she appreciated Joe's concern, Grace was fairly certain she could take care of herself now. Hadn't she proven it in the battle the other day? And she'd taken down the javelina single-handedly. With her knife tucked into the high, cuffed top of her moccasins and Joe's old holster on her hips, she could face whatever this town had to offer in a fair fight. She'd even become as fast a draw as Joe, so if it came to a shoot-out, she'd be ready.

Joe slowed his horse. He pulled closer to her and looked her straight in the eye. "No one in this town's going to hurt you, Grace Milton. I stake my life on it."

Grace's heart fluttered at the meaning in his eyes.

"And in any case, you don't need my help. They haven't seen what you can do with a gun or a knife or a rock now, right?"

Grace couldn't help grinning at his enthusiasm, but then she sobered. "It's true, I can take care of myself in a fair fight. But it's cowards like Behan that worry me. They wouldn't hesitate to shoot someone in the back."

She moved into tracking mode as they rode down the main street. Most people didn't give them a second glance, and Grace was glad Joe had dressed in the Mexican shirt and open black vest that many of the Ndeh had adopted. As for her, she'd donned buckskin leggings rather than the skirt, and had her braid tucked up under her Stetson. The buckskin top that Sequoyah had given her was decorated with beadwork, but until she got close, that wouldn't be visible. Still, once they got into the centre of town, all Grace's senses went into high alert. Her skin prickled as they neared the Bird Cage. Rather than avoiding it as her father had done, Joe rode up to it.

Grace's heart plummeted. Not only did she not want to walk through those doors, but her opinion of Joe fell along with her heart. They were there for supplies – she hadn't thought he was the kind to frequent bawdy houses. She kept her eyes averted so he wouldn't see the disappointment written in them.

"Hey," Joe said softly. "You all right?"

Grace gave a curt nod.

"You don't look all right."

I'm not, she wanted to burst out, but was afraid angry words would attract too much attention. She set her jaw and dismounted, tying Bullet next to Paint.

Joe put a hand on her arm, but Grace shook it off. She'd trusted him, and he knew what had happened to her in the Bird Cage. He obviously thought she wasn't a real lady.

"Grace?" Joe stepped in front of her and tilted her chin up, the way he did. She hoped that he wouldn't realize that the moisture stinging her eyes was a combination of anger and

225

disappointment. It could have come from the sand stinging them during the ride or from the too-bright sun…

"Hey. You know I wouldn't go in here unless I had to, right? But if we're going to trade, I have to meet some of the men. You don't have to go in if you don't want to. I don't blame you if you'd rather not accompany me, but I think we'd be safer together."

"What's wrong with the mercantile?" Grace murmured.

"That's fine if we pay, but we'll get a better deal trading with some of the men in here."

"You do know what this place is? It's called the Bird Cage Theatre." Grace spat out the last word. "But it's a…" She couldn't bring herself to say "house of ill-repute".

Joe's ears reddened, and he studied at the wooden walkway under their feet. "I know," he said softly. "But the sooner I get the business done, the sooner I can get out of there. Look, why don't you stay here with the horses?"

Grace bristled. She was just being silly – if she was going to make it on her own, she'd have to develop a thicker skin. If he went in there, then so would she. She straightened her spine. "No. It's OK. I'm coming with you."

Joe sighed. "You're right. The Bird Cage is no place for a woman."

"It's no place for a man either. Not a gentleman, at least," Grace snapped.

Joe hung his head. "I know. Believe me, I wouldn't go

anywhere near it if I didn't have to." He studied her. "Are you sure you want to do this?"

No, she wasn't. It was the last thing on earth she wanted to do, but Grace said brusquely, "Let's go." He was right – the faster they got it over with, the faster she could get out of town, and the faster she could get started on her mission. "Maybe with leggings and my braid under my hat, they'll mistake me for a man."

Joe looked her up and down, his eyes appreciative. "No chance of that unless they're blind or too drunk to see straight."

Grace's cheeks flamed, but Joe had already turned and was pushing open the door. The sickness in the pit of her stomach grew.

Joe waited for her to enter, then offered her an elbow protectively, as if he were a proper gentleman. Grace scanned the dark room for the sheriff. The last thing she wanted was for him to know she was back in town. But there was no sign Sheriff Behan. No Lil with the red feather bobbing in her hair either – although they could be in one of the cages overhead.

Grace headed for the darkest, farthest corner, one where she'd least likely be spotted by anyone coming in. The place was almost deserted before noon, but she was sure that, like the other bordello, things would get busier in the evening. A few men sat at tables scattered around the room, their chairs angled to get the best view of the girls serving drinks or singing and playing the piano. They took little notice as Grace sidled into a chair. Joe followed and sat so he blocked her from view of most of the room. He sat, tense and alert, examining each face as though looking for someone he knew would trade with them.

Grace did the same. None of the patrons looked familiar, except—

The man in the far corner sat hunched over a whisky, his hat pulled low over his eyes. He'd tucked his face down into his neckerchief so the lower part of his face was hidden except when he took a sip. As the whisky slid down his throat, something about the tilt of the hat, the set of the shoulders, and the man's sharp-nosed profile made Grace sit up and take notice.

His coat hung open, exposing two knives in his belt.

A chill ran through her.

He'd been there the night of her family's massacre. She'd swear it.

He was one of the Guiltless. He was the man who had – who had—

The memory of him unsheathing the knife blade was embedded in her memory. It brought back the sound of Daniel's surprised cry, then his body thudding to the ground. Sickness welled up in her. How dare this man sit here in public, drinking as if he had no conscience?

She had to do something.

CHAPTER TWENTY-ONE

"Joe?" Grace whispered.

He leaned close.

"That man over there." Grace nodded surreptitiously toward the whisky drinker. "He's one of them. I'm sure of it."

Joe's eyes widened. "One of the gang that killed—"

Grace's heart hardened, and she was sure it showed in her eyes. "Do me a favour," she interrupted, keeping her voice low. "Can you go over to his table? Get him talking? Find out more about him and who he is. Maybe he'll give away where the others are."

Joe shook his head. "What good would it do? Even if he's who you suspect he is, you can't shoot him in here."

Grace had already pulled her gun from the holster. She gripped it tightly underneath the table. "Who says?"

Joe reached over and removed her finger from the trigger. "You want to go to jail?" he hissed.

Rotting in jail would be worth it to get revenge for her brother's death. Only, if she did, she wouldn't be able to go after the rest of the gang. And the one she wanted most was their leader, Elijah Hale.

She finally slid the gun back into the holster and Joe's shoulders relaxed. He probably wouldn't have been so calm if he knew what she still had in mind, but first she had to be absolutely certain the man was the right one.

"Please," she said, looking at him imploringly. "For me?"

Joe's gaze wandered to her lips, then back to her eyes again. His Adam's apple bobbed up and down. "All right." He sighed. "I can't resist that face," he murmured as he shoved his chair back.

Did she hear him right? Grace stared at him as he strode across the room.

She cast furtive glances in the man's direction, trying not to seem too obvious, when Joe approached his table, two whiskies in hand. The man looked up, startled, when Joe spoke, but after Joe held out a glass, the man gestured to an empty chair. Joe sat in the chair the man indicated, plunked the whiskies down on the table, and slid one toward him.

Grace watched with narrow eyes as Joe beckoned for refills.

Every time the man's face lifted from the neckerchief, Grace became more and more certain she'd sighted her quarry.

She also kept a wary eye out for the sheriff or anyone else who might recognize her.

Across the room, she noticed that Joe barely touched the glass in front of him, but the man had knocked back three more drinks. He slumped farther and farther down in his chair and soon started listing to one side, then he'd jerk himself upright and sit stiffly for a few seconds, before leaning to the other side. He was drunker than a skunk, as Pa used to say – and his actions stunk worse than one too.

By the time Joe returned to her, his face was a mask of fury. "His name's Doc Slaughter," he spat, "and he's one of the Guiltless Gang, all right. After I plied him with a few drinks, he was only too happy to tell me about his exploits." Joe grimaced. "It was sickening to sit there and listen to him brag about his 'triumphs'. Says he used to be a dentist but turned to gambling and other ... activities as they paid more. If anyone deserves to be shot, it's him."

Grace's hand moved to her pistol.

Joe held out a hand. "No. I didn't mean by you." His voice grew hard. "The law should gun him down. From the way he's talking, he's on Wanted posters from here to Dodge. And all the way north into Minnie-soda, as he calls it."

"So why isn't he in jail?" Grace could barely force the words out through her gritted teeth.

Joe's jaw worked and his face contorted as if he'd love to strangle someone. "Why do you think?" he exclaimed. He glanced around to be sure no one had noticed his outburst, then he lowered his voice. "He had the nerve" – Joe's voice was tauter than a bowstring before letting an arrow fly – "to brag – *brag*, mind you – that he was safe here in Tombstone because the gang pays off the sheriff. All he has to do is watch out for the deputy, who's 'too law-abidin' fer his own good'." The anger in Joe's face was palpable. "But as the deputy never comes into this particular house of ill-repute, that varmint's pretty much safe."

Grace was so angry she was trembling. Doc Slaughter wasn't the only skunk around here. "So what are we going to do?"

Joe shook his head. "What *can* we do? He's under the sheriff's protection, and it seems most people in this town do what Sheriff Behan says, so they're not even going to report a known criminal, let alone take one down."

Grace already knew what cowards lived in this town. Not one of them had stood up for her, and the sheriff obviously had everyone under his thumb. It sickened her that Elijah Hale and his gang could get away with murder.

Joe gripped the edge of the table. "He even went so far as to say that if anyone even tried to take him down, the sheriff'd make them pay."

Grace clenched one hand into a fist. The other hovered over the gun, itching to draw it and shoot him, there and then.

In any other town, he'd be hanged. But here, he had free rein. He was free to kill. To murder innocent people and get away with it.

Joe laid a hand on Grace's shoulder. "I know how badly you want to shoot him, but that would be foolishness. Your life would be forfeit."

"*Someone* has to do it!"

"True, but that someone isn't you."

Grace exhaled, irritated. "Well, what about appealing to the deputy? Would he do his duty?"

"Let's find out. But first I need to get something to eat. I'm not used to drinking whisky and my head's spinning a little." Joe took a quick glance behind him. "That guy's so drunk, he won't be going anywhere for a while. If I understand rightly, the hardest part will be to get the deputy to come in here. He avoids this place like the plague. Plus if he knows the sheriff's in here somewhere, he'll figure Behan would do any necessary arresting."

"Yes, of course." Grace couldn't keep all the fury and sarcasm from her voice, but it softened as she turned to Joe. "Get something to eat and then we'll go to see the deputy."

"Will you be all right here for a short while? Seems like no one's paying attention to you, and the food here is truly awful. Most people are too drunk to notice, but I don't think I could stomach it. I might need to head out and get something."

"I'll be fine. I'll sit here and keep an eye on Doc…" She

couldn't bring herself to say the rest of the scumbag's moniker. "I'll watch him until you get back. Then we'll see that justice gets done. Whatever it takes," she added in a low murmur.

After Joe slipped out the door of the Bird Cage, Grace focused like a hawk on the bleary-eyed man. He slumped in his chair, head propped on his elbows, but still leered at the girls by the piano.

A young girl entered through the back door, carrying a stack of laundry, and Grace recognized her as the girl who'd brought her bathwater at the other bordello. As the girl trudged up the stairs with the heavy load, Doc's gaze followed her, and when she came back down, he perked up. He stood lurchingly and tottered toward her, but when the girl realized he was advancing on her, she backed away. He kept coming and she ducked out the back door.

Doc followed.

Grace didn't like the way he'd looked at that girl. He was up to no good, and she sure as heck wasn't about to let her quarry get away. Not when she was so close to justice. She jumped up and followed, pushing open the back door and finding herself in the alley by the stables. She glanced around and saw no one. Where had they gone?

Then she heard a cry coming from another alley beside the nearest stable. As Grace raced toward the sound, her braid tumbled from her hat and slapped at her shoulder.

Doc had pinned the girl down on some hay bales, and her

cries were piteous mewls.

His hand reached into his coat. "You be quiet or I'll slit your throat," he growled. A knife glinted in his hand.

In slow motion the pictures of that night flashed before Grace's eyes. That hand. That knife. The one that had killed her brother. One minute Daniel was charging past the root cellar. The next he lay in a bloody heap.

All the rage thundering through her made Grace snap. Her hand moved toward her holster. "Leave her alone or I'll shoot," she shouted.

The hand with the knife stilled, and Slaughter whipped his head around. But when he caught sight of Grace, he laughed loudly. "Little thing like you shouldn't be playing with guns." His words slurred together. Then a lecherous grin spread across his face, exposing a glinting gold tooth. "Want to join us, girlie?"

CHAPTER TWENTY-TWO

"I said… Let. Her. Go." The edge to Grace's voice was as sharp as a knife blade.

Bleary eyes raked her body. He ignored her. "What you doing dressed like a blasted injun?"

"Tracking you down," she snarled. "You killed my parents … my whole family. And you're going to pay."

His laugh was low and evil. "Ahhh," he drawled. "Thought I recognized you. You look just like yer ma."

Grace growled, the sound boiling up from deep within. "You keep my ma out of this. Now, let that girl go or I'll shoot."

Slaughter sneered. "You talk big, girlie, and I don't know where you got that gun but a little girl like you don't know how to use a weapon like that."

In one swift move, Grace stepped back and whipped out her revolver. "You sure about that?"

Slaughter pulled the girl over in front of him, and she whimpered in fright. With his free hand, he grabbed the girl's hair and wrenched her head back, exposing her neck. He touched the knife blade to the white skin and the girl squealed. The evil in Slaughter's laugh made Grace sick. He turned narrowed eyes toward Grace. "Drop that gun or I'll kill her."

The girl turned wide, pleading eyes towards Grace. Daniel's eyes would have held the same plea. A plea for mercy. A plea for someone to save him. A plea for life…

Sweat trickled down Grace's forehead and stung her eyes. *He killed Daniel*. And he wouldn't hesitate to kill again. The knife pressed closer in to the girl's pale throat.

Grace took a breath and time seemed to stop.

She squeezed the trigger.

As if in slow motion, the bullet left the gun, drilling straight toward Slaughter's forehead like the centre of a target. It hit, the impact knocking him backward. His mouth opened in shock for a second, then his arms released the girl as he crumpled to the ground.

The girl stumbled free, crying and gulping too much to get out coherent words. Between gasps, she managed, "Thank … you. Thank … you." Then, crying hysterically, her dress spattered with blood, she fled.

Grace waited for the smoke to clear. She stood over the body, gun pointed at Slaughter's chest, waiting for him to twitch, to move, to open his eyes. But he lay still.

As she knelt to see if he was still breathing, the eagle feather drifted from her hat and landed on the body. She reached down to retrieve it, but stopped. Perhaps it was fitting to leave it there. Cheis had said the eagle feathers stood for honour – she was defending her family's honour. She had six feathers: one for every member of the Guiltless Gang.

Now Grace vowed to pursue justice until a feather rested on each of the gang's lifeless bodies.

She didn't know how long she stood there before the sound of boots pounded down the alley.

"I heard a shot. Is everyone all—" The man skidded to a stop at the entrance of the stable. Grace turned, gun still in hand, to see Reverend Byington.

He stood at the end of the alley, shock in his eyes. "Are … are you all right, child?"

Was she all right? Grace wasn't sure. She couldn't stop the tremors wracking her body. "I-I killed him. I had to. He was going to—" She couldn't finish.

She'd wanted revenge and she'd gotten it. But the sense of triumph she expected to feel was buried under the sickness of killing another human being.

Another hand grabbed her shoulder. Grace jerked away and

whirled, raising her gun again.

Joe stared at her with shocked eyes. "What … what have you done?"

CHAPTER TWENTY-THREE

Joe grabbed her arm and glanced around the alleyway. "Did anyone else see you?"

Trembling from head to toe and sick to her stomach, Grace was too dazed to answer. She was sickened by what she'd done, but she also knew Slaughter deserved it. She had to save herself and the girl. But although she'd killed in the battle, this was different … uglier somehow. Something had happened inside her soul.

Wrapping an arm around her, Joe whisked Grace past the Reverend without a word, and around the corner into the back door of the Bird Cage. They almost bumped into the very girl Grace had saved as she stood huddled in the corner among the bags of stacked flour and supplies, shivering.

"She…" the girl said to Joe, grasping Grace by the hand. "She saved me."

Joe studied her. "Do you work here?" he said urgently. "Can you help us? She needs to clean up before anyone discovers what she's done." He motioned to the blood on Grace's hands and clothing. She hadn't even noticed it was there, and she thought hazily that it must have been from when she bent down over Slaughter's body.

The girl's voice was soft and shaky. "I just do the laundry for the Bird Cage."

Joe's voice was desperate. "She has to get cleaned up."

"I'll show her where the bath is." She turned to Joe. "They don't let men up there that haven't … paid."

He nodded. "I'll wait in the saloon. Just hurry."

The girl reached for Grace's arm. Her calloused palms were rough against Grace's skin. "I think I can get you water too." She peeked around the corner. "We just have to wait until Cora's back is turned." After a few moments, she said, "Quick now!" She dragged Grace toward a dark corner and a set of stairs, and they rushed past the rooms and entered a bathroom.

"Close the door and lock it. I'll stand guard out here."

A small, dirty looking-glass hung over the washstand in the corner. Grace stared at herself in the mirror, still in a daze. Her face was almost as pale white as the china pitcher and bowl except where it was smeared with Slaughter's blood from her fingers. Her blue eyes looked as cold and hard as ice, and there was a strange new glitter in her eyes.

Would she lose herself completely if she followed this path?

Grace shook her head. She'd started now and wouldn't be able to stop until justice had been meted out to every one of them, one way or another.

Hurriedly, she used the water in the pitcher to wash her face and scrub at the blood on her shirt and pants.

A commotion outside the door caused Grace's hand to stop mid-wipe.

"Outta the way, girlie. I gotta get in there."

"No." The girl's voice squeaked. She obviously wasn't used to standing up to people, and it showed in her voice.

"Whaddya mean, no?" The blustery voice struck fear into Grace's heart. That twang was unmistakable. Sheriff Behan. Grace's hand stilled. She'd killed one of his cronies and still had the bloodstains on her clothes. If he knew what she'd done…

Scuffling sounded outside the door. "Please, sir, someone's in there. An important person. They need privacy."

The sheriff laughed. "Paid you well, did they, to guard the door?"

The girl's voice came stronger now. "I promised not to let anyone disturb 'em."

"Problem, Johnny?" A woman's voice echoed down the hall.

"Damned girl won't let me in. Says there's an important

customer in there."

Lil's light laugh drifted through the door and squeezed Grace's gut. She glanced around. No place to hide unless she wedged herself behind the hip bath. But if Sheriff Behan opened that door, he'd discover her in seconds. Her heart in her throat, she pressed her ear to the door.

"Come on back to the room and get cleaned up," Lil called.

Grace took a breath as their footsteps receded down the hall.

Then the footsteps stopped and Lil's voice came again. "But you, girl, what are *you* doing up here?"

The girl stammered. "They stopped me downstairs and asked me to come up. I was only bringing the laundry, but they said I have to guard the door."

A silence, while Lil considered. "Make sure you give me half of what they give you."

"I-I will." The nervousness in her voice made Grace's heart ache.

Grace hurried back to the pitcher and scrubbed at the last of the spots. How would she get out of here and downstairs without Sheriff Behan seeing her? She'd done her best to get the worst of it cleaned up but all the dampness would be a dead giveaway.

When she'd smoothed her hair and washed her face, she peeked out the door. The palpable look of relief on the girl's face made Grace feel guilty.

243

"The sheriff," Grace whispered. "Where did he go?"

The girl pointed to a nearby room.

"I don't want him to know I was in here."

"Go quick then." She stationed herself outside the sheriff's room. "I'll try to distract him if he comes out."

Grace nodded.

Keeping one eye on the closed door, she hurried through the hall and down the steps. With relief, she spotted Joe sat in the back corner of the room, two glasses on the table in front of him.

"Sheriff Behan's upstairs."

Joe glanced toward the steps. "He doesn't know about Slaughter yet. But it won't be long. Might be best if he didn't see you looking like that."

Grace nodded. "We have to get out of here. Now."

Joe pushed one of the glasses toward her. "At least take a sip. It'll calm your nerves."

"What is it?" Grace picked up the glass and sniffed. Alcohol fumes almost choked her.

"Whisky."

Grace shook her head. "I don't need calming. I just need to get out of here."

The girl skulked down the steps. Seeing Grace, she rushed over. "If you want to avoid the sheriff, best go now."

"Thank you for all you've done."

The girl clasped Grace's hand in hers. "No! Thank *you*."

Grace suddenly thought of something. "Money. You'll need some money for Lil up there, to make it convincing, what you said…"

Unquestioningly, Joe brought out the pouch of silver and handed her two nuggets. "One for you and one for Lil."

The girl's eyes widened. "Oh, no, that's way too much."

"Then change it into cash and pay her what she'll think is fair."

The girl tried to hand one nugget back to Joe. "I can't take this much."

"Plenty more where that came from." Joe gave her a gentle push. "Best get back to work before you get in trouble."

The girl's eyes shone. "With this much, I won't need to go back to work for a long time."

Grace was stunned. Two nuggets of silver was a lot of money? And that woman at the bordello had taken the whole pouch. For one night's stay. Grace gritted her teeth. Sometime she'd go back and get her change. And how would she ever repay Joe for all the silver – and everything else – he'd given her? She knew she had to find a way to earn some money.

But right now they needed to get away.

"Let's get out of here before Sheriff Behan finds out what happened." Grace glanced down at her clothes. "But I need do something about my clothes. They're still damp." Her eyes lighted on the whisky glass. *Hmm…*

She made a show of bumping into the table so the whisky

245

glass splashed her clothes. A small puddle ran into her lap and onto the floor. Grace stood and wiped at her clothes, and the barmaid spotted her. She strode over with two rags, practically threw one at Grace without saying a word, and then mopped the table and floor with the other.

After the woman left, Joe hissed at Grace. "What'd you do that for? Now you smell like whisky. They'll think you were too drunk to hold your glass upright."

"Better that than realizing what the stains really are," she said, matter-of-fact.

Shock registered in Joe's eyes at her ruthlessness. "You've changed, Grace. What has happened to you?"

"I guess I grew up." She tried for bravado, but a memory of the alley and the sickness she'd felt returned. She pushed the thoughts away. "Let's go."

Just as they reached the back exit, the front door burst open. The deputy, badge shining on the lapel of his black cutaway coat, stood spreadeagled in the doorway.

"Someone shot Doc Slaughter in the back alley."

Gasps sounded around the room.

The deputy's eyes narrowed as he scanned the room. "I'm here for the one who did it."

CHAPTER TWENTY-FOUR

Grace started shaking so hard, Joe grasped her elbow and pinched it tight.

"Steady," he whispered.

They'd find her. Figure it out. She was done for. If they fled out the back door, the deputy would know she was guilty. And if she were running from the law, she'd never catch the rest of the Guiltless Gang.

"Brazen it out," Joe whispered.

All very well for him to say, but his finger wasn't the one that had pulled the trigger.

The deputy eyed each person in the room. One by one, they shook their heads. When his eyes rested on Grace, her heart pounded so hard she was sure he could hear. But his eyes slid past, dismissing her. He narrowed in on Joe.

"No witnesses to the deed far as I can tell. But a stable hand did mention someone with long hair and a black vest hustling in through the back door immediately afterward. Not saying that's the person what did it, but I'd like to talk to him…"

Grace clenched her hands into fists and willed her body to stop shaking. They couldn't question Joe. Both of them had to get out of here before the sheriff discovered her or before people figured who really shot the man. Only Reverend Byington might know what happened. And he, being a man of the cloth, would never lie. She had to disappear before the deputy found out.

"No one wants to claim the reward?" The deputy looked puzzled. "You kill one of the most wanted criminals in the nation and won't admit it?

Grace's eyes widened. *A reward?* Did that mean they wouldn't arrest her? She glanced at Joe with a question in her eyes.

"Reward?" one of the men at the bar bellowed. "There's a reward? Oh, uh, in that case, I'll own up. I shot him." He stood and puffed out his chest. "Reginald Black here. Best bounty hunter east of the Rockies."

Another man elbowed Reginald out of the way. "When did it happen, Deputy?"

"Best I ken tell, a few minutes ago."

"Reginald here was sitting at the bar when I came in a few minutes ago. That reward money's mine. I kilt him."

Another cowboy muscled him out of the way. "You couldn't shoot straight 'nuff to nick the side of a barn. That reward done belong to me."

"No, it don't."

The young girl's voice was shaky, but she spoke loudly enough to be heard over the excited buzz. "This here's who killed Slaughter." She pointed right at Grace.

Everyone whipped around to stare, then loud guffaws filled the room. "Purty little thing like that shot him?"

The deputy ignored her.

"She *did*," the girl insisted. "I swear it!"

The shouting and jostling in the bar reached a fever pitch, with several other men claiming the reward, shoving each other out of the way to get the deputy's attention.

Grace stepped forward and stared down all the men. "That's my money." She deserved that reward and she needed it. It would give her the funds to track down the rest of the gang, to pay Joe back. "I shot Slaughter."

Reginald laughed. "Go back home, little girl."

The wash-girl pointed to Grace and in a trembling but firm voice said, "This *little girl* saved my life. She shot that man in the alley."

The deputy shook his head, disbelieving.

Joe stepped up. "I was a witness. That reward belongs to her."

The murmurs around the room grew more heated. The man at the bar looked daggers at Grace, then gave a disgusted glance at Joe. "Hope you ain't gonna take the word of that dirty injun lover," he said to the deputy. He stood and placed a hand on his holster. "Ain't no way she could shoot nobody. Like to see the little girlie take me in a fast draw. She don't even look like she can hold a gun steady!"

"Oh yeah?" Grace said, her eyes narrowing.

"Yeah…" He eyed the gun in her holster. "One, two, three," he shouted and drew.

But Grace's gun was already in her hand.

"Woo-wee," one of the old-timers at the bar gloated. "You got outdrawn by a little girl."

"Lucky draw," the man said through gritted teeth. "She probably don't have any idea how to shoot that thing."

"Wanna bet?"

Before he could respond, Grace's shot blasted across the bar. Her bullet dug into the wooden floor right in front of his feet, showering splinters over his boots. She blew the black smoke from the tip of her gun. "Next time I'll aim higher."

"Hey! What's going on down there?" Sheriff Behan's voice cracked loudly from above. He leaned over the railing of one of the cages, his bolo tie askew. He ran a hand over his mussed hair.

"Trying to find out who deserves the reward for killing Doc Slaughter," the deputy informed him.

"Reward? Someone *killed* Doc Slaughter?" Sheriff Behan clutched at his throat. "When?" He looked sick.

"Few minutes ago out in the alley." The deputy shook his head. "We got at least three people what claim to have done it." He motioned to the man at the bar. "Reginald, Tex, and—" He couldn't keep the sneer from his face as he pointed at Grace. "That lil gal over there."

The anger pulsing from the sheriff's eyes frightened Grace, but she gave him a defiant glare.

"My bet's on Tex," the sheriff said, but anger mixed with fear made his voice shake. "But I don't cotton to any shooting in this town—"

The doors behind the deputy swung open. Everyone froze in place. Reverend Byington entered and looked startled at the tableau.

He spotted Grace and headed toward her. "Are you all right now, child?"

Grace nodded, but couldn't shake the fear that had gripped her at the message underlying the sheriff's gaze. He'd make her pay. Maybe she should let Tex claim the reward and hightail it out of here. She backed up a step.

The Reverend suddenly seemed to realize that everyone in the room was not moving. He glanced around. "What's going on?"

The deputy replied, "Trying to find out who shot Doc Slaughter in the back alley, but it seems we have some

251

conflicting stories."

Reverend Byington opened his mouth, looked at Grace, and then closed it.

"Well, maybe now that you're here, Reverend, we might get some honest answers. Who wants to swear on the Good Book?" The deputy turned to Reverend Byington. "Somehow no one claimed responsibility for the killing until I done mentioned a reward. Then they was all too happy to claim it."

"A reward?" Byington's voice had a cautious edge to it.

"Yep." The deputy squared his shoulders. "I already sent a Pony Express rider to the governor, telling him we took down one of the most dangerous criminals in the whole US of A."

"So the person responsible would be a hero rather than a criminal?"

"Absolutely."

Overhead, Sheriff Behan growled deep in his throat. Reverend Byington looked up. "Is that right, Sheriff?"

Behan's hands clenched the railing and it was obvious he was forcing out words. "If the deputy alerted the governor, then yes, the shooter would be" – his throat clenched convulsively – "a hero."

"In that case," Byington announced with a smile, "I'd be glad to tell you the truth. I was an eyewitness."

Tex slumped onto his bar stool, muttering. Reginald's face turned red and he clamped his hat onto his head, hiding his face.

The Reverend gestured toward Grace. "That young lady

252

shot him in self-defence."

Murmurs broke out around the room.

"She's only a girl."

"She couldn'ta done it. No way."

"But she did beat Tex to the draw."

"Only cos he's drunk."

Grace strode toward the deputy, her hand outstretched. "My reward money, please."

The deputy handed her a heavy sack.

"What's that yer giving her?" the sheriff demanded.

The deputy smiled up at him. "Saw that stash of silver dollars when you opened yer desk drawer. Figured the governor's good for the money, so he'll pay you back. Hope that was all right."

The sheriff growled again and his face grew so red Grace thought he might explode. His glare promised he'd track her down and get revenge.

But it gave her an idea.

She wasn't cut out for typical "woman's work". A barmaid or a seamstress? No.

But bounty hunting?

Bounty hunters made money. And she'd learned so much from Joe about how to track and shoot – they were what she was truly good at. If she became a bounty hunter, she could do two things – get revenge for her family and make the world safe from criminals, so no one else would have to live through what she had. She'd track down the Guiltless Gang but she'd be glad to help anyone else who needed her.

Grace cleared her throat and hoped she wasn't making the biggest mistake of her life.

"If this is the calibre of bounty hunters available in these parts, I'm throwing my hat in the ring," she said loudly. "Anyone need a criminal tracked down, I'm putting myself out there for hire."

Behind her Joe gasped. "What?"

But Grace moved through the crowd with confidence, ignoring the derisive laughter, the catcalls, and the cloud of doubt that hung in the air. She'd found her calling. Her purpose. She would not only avenge her family's deaths, she'd do this in their honour. Clear this town of criminals, and make a living doing it.

Reverend Byington's eyes contained a mixture of pride and sadness as Grace passed him carrying her reward. She smiled at him. The pastor had his ideas about God, but his Good Book also said, "An eye for an eye, a tooth for a tooth." And she was going to bring her own brand of justice to the West.

Maybe, given time, she'd be able to forgive and trust God again, but for now she had her mission. And no one and nothing would stop her.

Not Sheriff Behan. Not the townspeople. Not Reverend Byington. And not Joe.

She'd work alone.

CHAPTER TWENTY-FIVE

Joe followed her outside, shaking his head.

"The sheriff, did you see his face?" Grace hugged the bag and shot a nervous glance toward the door of the Bird Cage. Would the sheriff come storming out?

"He's not happy, that's for sure," Joe said tightly.

"He's furious." She couldn't help but smile. She stared at the sack as they hurried down the alley to the stables. "Think this is his pay-off money?" The thought made her want to throw the money down, but then she laughed. "Actually, I guess it's payback. The sheriff paid me for taking down one of the Guiltless Gang. Very fitting."

Joe grinned along with her but quickly grew sober. "Can't

that be enough for you?" But he asked it as if he already knew the answer.

Grace looked at him for a long minute. With what happened to his parents, she'd thought he, of all people, would finally understand.

After they'd saddled their horses, Grace drew out a pile of silver dollars. "That's for you."

"I didn't do anything to deserve it."

"You gave *me* a bag of silver. I can't pay you what that's really been worth, but consider this a down payment."

"You don't owe me anything." Joe started to mount, then stopped. "In all this madness, I forgot that we have errands to run!"

They led their horses to the mercantile, keeping a watch for Sheriff Behan. Grace bought small gifts for everyone. A bag of penny candy for Sequoyah, some patent medicine and healing tonics for Cheveyo, a bright bandana for Cheis. She added some small gifts and toys for the women and children. She selected a shiny apple for Bullet. But what could she get for Joe?

When he admired a Smith and Wesson revolver, she put it on the counter along with bullets.

Joe raised his eyebrows. "Giving up on the Colt?"

"Nope." Grace tried to put some sass in her tone so he wouldn't guess why she was buying it. "I figure a bounty hunter should have more than one weapon." She added plenty of bullets for the Colt.

Joe frowned. "You weren't serious about that bounty hunter stuff, were you?"

Grace put her hands on her hips. "You think I can't do it?"

"I have no doubt you can. The question is, should you? Don't … don't go to the dark side, Grace," he pleaded.

"Since when is capturing criminals going to the dark side?"

Joe ignored her and continued heaping the goods Cheis had requested on the counter, but then he turned and looked her straight in the eye. "I get the impression you don't aim to *capture* them."

Grace turned away from his probing gaze. "I'll do whatever I have to do."

"That's what I was afraid of." Joe handed over the pelts and deerskins to the shopkeeper. "Most likely no one will hire a girl anyway," he muttered so quietly that Grace almost didn't catch it – but she did.

She clenched her teeth. *Maybe not.* But that didn't mean she couldn't try.

As soon as they'd made their purchases, they galloped off, Grace still keeping a wary eye behind her for the sheriff. After they'd made to the outskirts of town, she took a deep breath. Maybe he really wasn't coming after them.

But a short while later hoof beats pounding behind them made Grace's heart speed up. She turned to see Reverend Byington riding toward them. The tension that had coiled inside her relaxed.

"Well, Grace, I was so hoping to have a chance to talk to you. Although not under these circumstances," the Reverend gasped as he caught up to them.

Grace reined Bullet to a walk so the preacher could catch his breath.

Reverend Byington seemed to be struggling for words. "About today… I'm sure what happened was an accident. Self-defence?"

His look made Grace squirm. It was as if he could see clear through to her soul. His eyes held both compassion and a warning.

"Trying to play God can jeopardize your soul, Grace Milton. Only God should decide a man's fate."

Joe burst out, "I've been telling her that. And that she needs to let go of her anger and find peace!"

"Sounds like you're a good influence, son."

Would everyone stop talking as if she weren't here?

The preacher turned toward Grace. "I know mere words won't stop you, but look to the light rather the dark." He reached into the bag slung over his shoulder. "I'd planned to ride out and give you this." He withdrew a square object wrapped in a handkerchief and held it out.

Grace didn't reach for it. She only shook her head. "You've done too much for me already."

The preacher smiled. "It's not a gift. It belongs to you."

Grace unrolled the fabric. There in her hand was the tintype, with her family's faces staring out at her. Her eyes filled with tears. "I … I thought I'd never see this again. Thank you, thank you, thank you…"

"Don't thank me. Thank *God* that I found it. I'd started back toward town but knew I'd never rest until I knew you were safe at the Joneses. I rode back to accompany you and saw that glinting under the mesquite tree." He gave her a stern look. "I searched for hours, but never found you. I hoped that nothing had happened to you."

"I actually never went to their cabin," Grace confessed. "The Ndeh took me in." If she hadn't gotten lost, she might have run into Reverend Byington and she'd now be stuck at the Joneses. Instead she'd been through some ordeals, but she'd remained free and now had the skills to take care of herself.

The preacher pursed his lips. "The Ndeh are good people … but you should be in a real home."

Joe sat up straighter. "The Ndeh have *given* her a real home."

"I'm sure they have, son. I only meant a home where she'll get some teaching from the Good Book."

Silence descended for a minute. Grace wanted to rail against that but the preacher had been nothing but kind. She kept silent.

The preacher took a deep breath. "Well, now that you have money, I hope you'll consider settling down."

Grace looked away. She couldn't meet his eyes and say what she had to say. She didn't want to read the disappointment in them. She hugged the tintype to her chest with her free hand.

But before she could say anything, Joe said, "We're taking good care of her, sir."

"Very well. I'll be out to check on both of you from time to time. But, Grace, every time you look at that photograph, remember that you came from *love*, not hatred or vengeance."

Grace nodded. He'd given her back her most prized possession; she could give him a promise in return.

"I'll try to remember that."

Reverend Byington's grin might not have been so broad if he'd known her plans, but Grace would keep them to herself. Whenever she spoke of them, she met only opposition.

The preacher wheeled his horse around. "I need to head back now, but I'll be praying for both of you." He laughed. "You know what you should be called? Amazing Grace. Do you know the hymn?" He broke into song, and the sound of his deep bass echoed after them as they sped up the hill to camp.

CHAPTER TWENTY-SIX

The sun was sinking fast by the time they made it back. Sequoyah came racing toward them and grabbed Grace by the arm as she dismounted from Bullet. She pointed toward her father's *kuugh'a*, where another horse was staked.

"You want to show me you got a new horse?" Grace said, confused.

"No, No." Sequoyah seemed close to tears. "It's… It's Tarak's."

Grace didn't understand why Sequoyah sounded so desperate.

Joe's deep voice broke in. "Grace doesn't know all our customs yet."

Grace noticed he said "our". Despite what he'd said, she realized he really did feel a part of them. That's where they were different. As much as she loved the Ndeh, Grace needed to strike out on her own.

"When a man stakes a horse outside a girl's home," Joe explained, "he's asking to marry her. She has four days to respond. If she feeds and waters the horse, she's agreed to be his wife. If she does not want the man, she does not care for the horse."

Sequoyah's voice was tight with panic. "I cannot leave a horse without food and water for four days. But I do not want to say yes."

"What is your heart telling you to do?" Grace asked gently.

Sequoyah looked confused.

Joe translated, but then he shuffled his feet and looked uncomfortable. "I think this is girl talk. I'll go unload the horses."

Sequoyah waited until Joe had left. Then she clasped her hands against her chest. "I only love Dahana."

"Then you must turn down Tarak."

"Dahana must care for his family. He is not ready for a wife."

"Wait for him," Grace urged.

"But my father say Tarak is good hunter and warrior. Tarak take the most scalps in battle."

"But you don't love him. Follow your heart."

"Like you?

Sequoyah glanced over to where Joe was unloading the horses.

Grace pulled her gaze away and shook her head. "That's different."

"I not understand. You love him, do you not?"

"I... It's complicated. Besides, Joe hasn't asked me to marry him." Grace had to change the subject. "*You're* the one who must decide."

Sequoyah's face took on a troubled expression. "If I feed the horse too soon, everyone will say I too eager. If I wait too long, I look cruel. So I must decide by tomorrow."

"Follow your heart," Grace repeated, thumping her chest.

"It not easy."

She grimaced. "It never is."

Sequoyah studied Grace more closely now. "You look different."

Grace didn't want to get into the whole story. She only nodded. "That reminds me, I've got something for you." She held out the gifts from the mercantile. "This is for you. And these are for everyone in camp to share."

Sequoyah hugged her. "Oh! Thank you." Her face saddened. "You are … going?"

Grace nodded, swallowing hard. "I'll miss you, Sequoyah. Thank you … for everything." With a heavy heart, she turned and started to walk away.

263

"Wait, Grace!" Sequoyah called and ran after her. She lifted a shell and bear-claw necklace over her head and draped it around Grace's neck. "To show we be friends forever, we give gift from heart. I remember you always. You remember me?"

Grace hugged her. "I'll never forget you, Sequoyah. Never." *And maybe someday we'll meet again.*

The sun had almost disappeared below the horizon. Grace wished she could ride off now but it would be safer to wait until morning. She wandered around the camp, silently saying farewells. When she passed the new medicine lodge, Cheveyo called out to her. Grace went over, and he motioned for her to join him inside.

When she gave him his gift, he rewarded her with a broad smile. "I can see if white man's medicine is as good as ours."

"I'm sure it won't be." Grace pulled up her sleeve. Her scar had faded to a thin line. "You healed me. And Bullet is all better too, thanks to you."

"I am glad to help." Then Cheveyo's face grew serious. "I, too, have a gift for you. I have waited for … the right time." He moved to one of the baskets and drew out a handful of pouches. Then he sat down in front of her and looked deeply into her eyes.

"Dyami, you are going on a journey. You will travel far.

Not only your body will walk this path but your spirit too. The way will be hard and you will face much danger. You must be ready for what lies ahead. And you must learn to listen to your *heart*."

Grace sat quietly, taking in his words.

Cheveyo waited, letting his stillness speak to her soul. Then he pointed to the pouches. He explained what each ointment and herb did, and how to apply them. Grace accepted them gratefully – she'd seen what powerful medicine Cheveyo had. And she would remember his words of wisdom.

By the time she had handed out the rest of the gifts, the moon had risen and the camp had a subdued air. No dancing or drumming. People still walked around with sadness in their eyes. But mothers hugged their children close and smiled at Grace. They all murmured words of appreciation as she passed. But the one person she most wanted to see was nowhere to be found.

With a heavy but determined heart, Grace gathered all her belongings and headed off to find Joe. Using her tracking instincts, she mounted the rise to the pasture, her steps so soft that Joe didn't hear her. His back was facing her and he was staring off toward the town far below, just as she herself had done so many times these past weeks. A few lights glowed in the distance, but most of the light came from the moon and the stars dancing overhead.

Grace knew this might be this last time she'd ever see him, and she wanted to keep this memory with her forever. She watched him for a long while, imprinting every detail in her mind. Then, her voice soft so as not to startle him, she called his name.

Joe turned and looked at her, taking in her belongings slung over her shoulder.

"So this is it?" He kicked at a clod of dirt at his feet.

He looked so crestfallen that it broke Grace's heart. If she didn't have her parents' deaths to avenge, that look alone would have convinced her to stay.

He walked over to her slowly and reached for her hand, a sad smile on his face. "You don't have to go, you know that."

"Why would I stay, when you'll be going yourself? The Restless One, that's what they call you, right?" She tried for a smile, but failed. "If I stayed and you left, I'd feel … I don't know…" Grace lowered her eyes. She couldn't say what was in her heart.

"I'd stay if you did." Joe tilted her chin and gazed deep into her eyes. "Think about it."

Then he leaned toward her. This time Grace didn't close her eyes and wait and hope. Sequoyah's advice came back to her. *You kiss* him.

She stepped closer and gently brushed her lips to his. But

266

it was like kissing stone; his mouth didn't move. Embarrassed, Grace started to pull away, but then Joe's arms encircled her fiercely, pulling her close as if he never wanted to let her go.

Their lips pressed together, moving rhythmically, their hearts beat as one.

It was everything Grace had dreamed it would be and more.

When they finally broke apart, Joe ran a finger across her lips. "I could go with you…?"

The question hung between them as they settled on the grass, Joe's arm around her, her head on his shoulder. They stayed like that until Grace began to shiver.

"You cold?" Joe nuzzled her neck and wrapped both arms around her.

When Grace nodded, he reluctantly pulled away from her, stood, and gathered firewood. She admired his broad back as he bent and piled the wood, then twirled two sticks together until sparks lit the dried grasses he'd used for kindling. Then he bent and blew gently until smoke rose and flames licked the wood. He made it look easy, she thought wryly, and a mix of emotions jumbled in her chest.

Thanks to Joe, she now *could* light a fire, but she still didn't have all his expertise. It would be good to have him alongside her. It would be the best of both worlds, and it meant she wouldn't have to leave him.

But would she be able to concentrate on her mission? And could she let her heart get entangled when she'd vowed never to love anyone again?

Even more importantly, would he prevent her from doing what she *had* to do?

Joe settled back down beside her next to the fire and pressed his lips to hers again. As they kissed, Grace wanted it to last forever. She never wanted to leave this spot. They sat for hours, holding each other close, staring at the sky, the vast blackness overhead dotted with pinpricks of light. Then when they finally tired, they lay down, cuddled together for warmth as the fire died down to embers, and drifted off to sleep under the stars…

When dawn broke, Grace awoke and slid out of Joe's arms. She gathered her things and loaded them onto Bullet. Eyes misty, she stood for a long time debating, taking in every detail of Joe's rugged, handsome face as he slept soundly. Her heart twisted painfully at the thought of leaving him.

If she woke him to say goodbye, she'd never be able to go.

But, tears in her eyes, she couldn't resist kneeling and pressing a feather-light kiss to his forehead. Joe stirred and murmured something in his sleep. Then Grace laid the Smith and Wesson revolver beside him, wishing she had something more to give him for all he'd given her.

With one last backward glance at his sleeping figure, she

mounted Bullet, turned him in the opposite direction, and quickly galloped away. Deep inside, she vowed that someday, some way, when justice was done, she'd find her way back here to the place where her heart belonged.

But for now, she needed to do this alone.

Other books in the **WANTED** series

GRACE ALONE

Can Grace make it on her own as a bounty hunter?

Leaving Joe behind has given Grace a new kind of heartache, adding to the loss of her family. She decides to become a bounty hunter, despite it being 'no life for a woman'. It will help her track down the Guiltless Gang, as well as paying the rent.

Her first test is a criminal known as the Black Coat, who's been preying on vulnerable women. She's about to put a dangerous plan into action when Joe comes into her life again, showing her what life could be like if she let go of revenge.

Then, as she struggles with her feelings, the Guiltless Gang appear tantalizingly close…

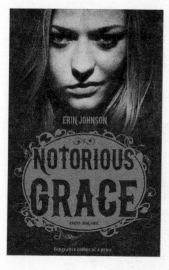

NOTORIOUS GRACE

The desire for revenge will not stay buried.

Grace is slowly rebuilding her life: she's gaining a reputation as a bounty hunter and tentatively courting Joe. Then attractive fellow bounty hunter Kyle Black comes to town with shocking news: he's killed Guiltless Gang member Bloody Kit Doolan. It's what she wanted, so why doesn't she feel like justice has been served?

GRACE AVENGED

Justice is almost within Grace's grasp…

As Grace's relationship with Joe heals, she gets a lead on her most prized target – Guiltless Gang leader, Elijah Hale. And he's not alone. Together with his mistress and fellow gang-member Bella, Hale has been scamming his way across Arizona, with Bella posing as a travelling medium.

This time, revenge may cost Grace the ultimate price.

For more exciting books from brilliant
authors, follow the fox!
www.curious-fox.com